"Mr. Walsh, what Patrick ... *his father."*

Peter squared his shoulders, a bit of his temper returning. Obviously, he took her last comment as an indictment. "I'll talk to him tonight. You won't have problems with his behavior again."

Lisa's heart sank. Had he heard her at all?

Peter Walsh, his square jaw tight and his back stiff, turned to stalk out of the conference room.

"Mr. Walsh, I—"

But he was gone. All six feet plus of seething testosterone and brooding eyes. Lisa inhaled deeply, hoping to calm her frazzled nerves, but instead drew in the enticing scents of leather and pine that Peter Walsh left in his wake.

She had no business thinking of her student's father in the terms that filtered through her head—sexy, virile—but with a man like Peter Walsh, how could she not?

Dear Reader,

Having contributed to The Coltons: Family First continuity that came out in 2008, I fell in love with all of the Colton clan. Naturally, I was thrilled when I was asked to write a book for the newest Colton series.

In *P.I. Daddy's Personal Mission,* Peter Walsh puts his private-detective skills to work searching for answers to his father's murder. He's convinced Mark Walsh will never have justice as long as a Colton is in charge of the investigation! But his private investigation gets sidetracked by personal issues, namely his son's need for fatherly guidance and an attractive schoolteacher who wants to give him lessons in matters of the heart.

I hope you'll enjoy this latest installment of The Coltons of Montana, and be sure to come back next month when Karen Whiddon wraps the whole story up! Watch, too, for my third Bancroft Brides book early next year. I love to hear from readers. You can write to me through my website, www.bethcornelison.com.

Have a blessed Thanksgiving, and happy reading!

Beth Cornelison

BETH CORNELISON

P.I. Daddy's Personal Mission

ROMANTIC
SUSPENSE

Special thanks and acknowledgment to
Beth Cornelison for her contribution
to The Coltons of Montana miniseries.

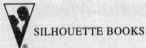

SILHOUETTE BOOKS

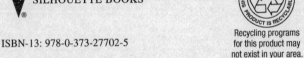

Recycling programs
for this product may
not exist in your area.

ISBN-13: 978-0-373-27702-5

P.I. DADDY'S PERSONAL MISSION

Copyright © 2010 by Harlequin Books S.A.

Books by Beth Cornelison

Silhouette Romantic Suspense

To Love, Honor and Defend #1362
In Protective Custody #1422
Danger at Her Door #1478
Duty to Protect #1522
Rancher's Redemption #1532
Tall Dark Defender #1566
★*The Christmas Stranger* #1581
Blackout at Christmas #1583
    "Stranded with the Bridesmaid"
★*The Bride's Bodyguard* #1630
P.I. Daddy's Personal Mission #1632

★The Bancroft Brides

BETH CORNELISON

started writing stories as a child when she penned a tale about the adventures of her cat, Ajax. A Georgia native, she received her bachelor's degree in public relations from the University of Georgia. After working in public relations for a little more than a year, she moved with her husband to Louisiana, where she decided to pursue her love of writing fiction.

Since that first time, Beth has written many more stories of adventure and romantic suspense and has won numerous honors for her work, including a coveted Golden Heart award in romantic suspense from Romance Writers of America. She is active on the board of directors for the North Louisiana Storytellers and Authors of Romance (NOLA STARS) and loves reading, traveling, Peanuts' Snoopy and spending downtime with her family.

She writes from her home in Louisiana, where she lives with her husband, one son and two cats who think they are people. Beth loves to hear from her readers. You can write to her at P.O. Box 5418, Bossier City, LA 71171 or visit her website at www.bethcornelison.com.

To my parents—
thanks for all you do!

And in memory of Samson, our lovable goofball,
who exuded awesomeness into our lives and left
three big paw prints on our hearts.
You are missed.

Chapter 1

His father had been murdered—*twice*.

Peter Walsh ground his back teeth together and shifted uncomfortably in the front seat of his truck. Stakeouts were tedious enough without nagging concerns over a crime that should never have happened. His father had been killed fifteen years ago—or so his family had thought. But then, just a few months ago, Mark Walsh's body had been found in Honey Creek. All evidence pointed to murder. A *recent* murder.

So where had Mark Walsh been for the last fifteen years if he was not dead? Who had known Peter's father was still alive and hated him enough to murder him—again?

Explaining to his son, Patrick, that Grandpa Walsh had been murdered—for real this time—had confused and upset the impressionable ten-year-old. Peter could see the strain all of the turmoil was causing Patrick. He'd become withdrawn, sullen. One more concern to keep Peter awake at night.

Peter rubbed warmth into his cold hands. The November morning was brisker than average thanks to the cold front that had dumped several inches of snow overnight. The first signs of winter had come to Honey Creek, Montana, with a snowfall in October. But that snow had been followed by unseasonably warm weather, a tornado and then more cold air. Peter shook his head, musing over the crazy seesawing weather.

Raising his camera with its telephoto lens to the open truck window—a necessity for a clear view despite the frigid temperatures—Peter focused on the front porch, then the barn door, of the Rigsby residence. Still no activity. Still no proof that Bill Rigsby was defrauding his insurance company with false injury claims.

With his surveillance of Rigsby's farm yielding little evidence to take back to his client, Peter's thoughts returned to the numerous troubling events his family had dealt with in recent months, the most glaring being the shocking reappearance and murder of his father. Peter's stomach rumbled, and he lifted his travel mug to sip coffee that had long ago gotten cold. Maybe he should pack it in, get some lunch and head to the hospital to visit Craig.

When a woman stepped out on the Rigsbys' porch to feed a pair of mutts, he lifted the camera again. He clicked a few shots, just because, as his thoughts mulled the latest hit the Walshes had taken.

Craig Warner, the man who had been more of a father to Peter than Mark Walsh had ever been, had suffered his own mysterious attack in the last few weeks. The stomach virus Craig thought he had turned out to be arsenic poisoning. Lester Atkins, Craig's assistant, had tried to kill the CFO of Walsh Enterprises within months of Mark Walsh's murder.

Then his sister Mary had been blatantly run off the road after visiting Damien Colton in prison. Coincidence?

Not likely.

Peter's gut tightened. He smelled a conspiracy. The Walsh family, the people he cared about, were under attack. Someone in Honey Creek had viciously—

Click-click.

Peter froze as the pumping sound of a shotgun filtered into the open truck window.

"Who the hell are you and what are you doin' on my land?" a low voice growled.

Peter turned slowly, his hands up, and stared down the barrel of a Remington 870. Silently he cursed the distracting thoughts that had allowed this armed farmer to approach his truck without Peter noticing. That kind of inattention could get him killed. An unsettling thought when the Walshes and their business associates seemed to be the target of a murderer.

Peter took a slow breath that belied the speed of his thoughts as he analyzed the best way to diffuse this situation. "Is that a Wingmaster?"

The armed farmer lowered the muzzle an inch or so to narrow a curious gaze on Peter. "Yeah."

Peter smiled. "Man, I've been wanting to buy a Wingmaster for years. Remington sure knows how to build a beauty of a shotgun, don't they?"

The farmer hesitated then snarled, "I asked you who the hell you were! What are you doin' out here?"

Peter's pulse kicked. The last thing he needed was an irate farmer with a twitchy trigger finger blasting a hole in his truck—or his head. Palms out in a conciliatory gesture, Peter tried again to calm the man. "If you'll put the gun down, we'll talk. I don't want any trouble."

The man shifted his weight nervously. "Get out of the truck."

Hell. If he got himself killed, who'd raise Patrick? His motherless son had already lost too many people in his short life. Peter gritted his teeth. Screwups like this weren't like him. Proof positive that he needed to get the disarray of his private life in order before he could be effective for his clients.

He nodded his compliance before he reached down to open the driver's door of his truck. As he stepped down from the cab, he resisted the urge to stretch his stiff muscles. Better not give the jittery farmer any reason to shoot. As he slid out of the truck, he pulled his identification wallet out of the map pocket and flipped it open.

If people didn't look too closely, his private-investigator license looked pretty intimidating.

"I'm Peter Walsh, and I'm here on official business." The vague statement usually made people think he meant *police* business, which won their cooperation.

The farmer looked skeptical. He wouldn't be bluffed. "What kind of official business?"

Peter wasn't about to show his hand until he could determine whether the farmer was likely to report to the Rigsbys on Peter's surveillance operation. If Rigsby had a heads-up that the insurance company was on to his fraud, he could cover his tracks. Peter needed to catch the man who claimed to have a disabling injury in the act—horseback-riding, snowmobiling, shoveling his front sidewalk. Anything that would prove he wasn't bedridden with a back injury as he claimed.

"Lower the gun, and we'll talk."

Farmer tensed. "I'm giving the orders here, buddy. You've been sittin' out here on my property for hours, and I want to know why. Now!"

Technically the road was county property, but Peter didn't feel quibbling over that point was wise, given the man's mood. And his weapon.

Peter's priority was getting the shotgun barrel out of his face. He was already plotting his next move as he asked, "We had reports of some suspicious activity at your neighbors' house. When was the last time you saw Bill Rigsby?"

"Bill Rigsby? What kind of suspicious—?"

Peter made his move.

While the farmer's attention was focused on answering the baited question, Peter swept his arm up, knocking the shotgun away from his face, then followed through by grabbing the gun by the barrel and yanking it from the startled farmer's grip.

"Hey!" the man shouted.

Peter tossed the weapon on the front seat of his truck and slammed the door. "I asked you to lower the gun. You didn't, so now we'll do things my way. You'll get the gun back once you answer *my* questions."

The farmer stepped closer, glowering, but his nose only reached Peter's chin. "You sonofa—"

"Answer the question!" Peter barked, seizing the upper hand. He loomed over the shorter man, squaring his broad shoulders and narrowing a hard stare. "When was the last time you saw Bill Rigsby?"

The farmer's Adam's apple bobbed. "Yesterday."

"What was he doing?"

The farmer shrugged. "Nothing. Just out riding, checking his fence."

"On horseback?"

The man gave him a no-shit-Sherlock look. "Yeah. Horseback. Why?"

Peter kept his expression blank, although he sensed the

farmer could prove a wealth of information. The sooner he finished the Rigsby case for his client, the sooner he could look into the questions surrounding his father's murder. "Does Rigsby ride often?"

The farmer cocked his head, sending Peter a dubious frown. "He has to. Got a farm to run."

Peter catalogued the information, then hooked his thumbs in his jeans pockets. "Ever see him shoveling snow?"

The farmer snorted. "There a law against that?"

"No. Does he shovel the front walk or does his wife?"

"He does. Why does that matter? What kind of suspicious activity is he into?"

To keep Rigsby's neighbor off balance, Peter asked, "You ever see a black van parked in front of Bill's house?"

The farmer took a step back and squinted at Peter with deep creases in his brow. Lowering his voice, the farmer asked, "Is he dealing drugs?"

Deflecting the question and turning it to his advantage, Peter responded, "Why? Have you seen evidence that Rigsby has acquired a large unexplained sum of money recently?"

The other man folded his arms over his chest and frowned. "Well, he did buy a new four-wheeler a couple of weeks ago. My wife and I were puzzling over how he afforded it, what with the economy being the way it is and all." He shook his head, his scowl darkening. "Are you telling me Bill Rigsby is a drug dealer?"

Peter raised a palm, keeping his expression neutral. He'd feed the farmer's paranoia without outright lying if it would get him the information he needed. "Let's not get ahead of ourselves. My investigation isn't finished." He glanced meaningfully toward the Rigsby property. "Do you have any idea where I might find Bill Rigsby now?"

The man lifted one shoulder. "Can't say for sure, but I think I heard him and his son leave by snowmobile at first light this morning. My guess is they headed down to the south pasture for the day."

Peter blew out a deep breath that clouded in front of him in the chilly November air. "So Bill's still able to drive a snowmobile since his injury?"

The farmer looked confused. "What injury? Did that good-for-nothing liar tell someone he was laid up again?"

Bingo.

"Again?" Peter eyed the man carefully. "He's pulled a scam before?"

"And brags about it." The farmer glared in the direction of the Rigsby farm. "I hate cheaters."

"If you knew your neighbor was involved in the kind of insurance fraud that means you have to pay higher premiums, would you be willing to testify at a deposition on behalf of the insurance company?"

The man arched an eyebrow. "Testify?"

"That you've seen him shoveling snow, horseback-riding and snowmobiling."

The farmer jerked a nod. "Damn straight."

Peter turned and took the shotgun out of his truck. He handed it back to the farmer. "Is there a road that will take me to the Rigsbys' south pasture? I'd like to get a few pictures of Bill Rigsby snowmobiling."

The farmer gave Peter a gloating grin. "There sure is."

An hour later, Peter drove toward the hospital in Honey Creek to see Craig Warner. He had a dozen or more incriminating photos of Bill Rigsby and his son riding snowmobiles, chopping wood and loading hay bales in the south pasture. More than enough evidence for his client to prove that Rigsby's disability claim was false. With that matter behind him, Peter focused his attention on the problems that had kept him awake at night in recent weeks—the attacks on his family.

While he hadn't been close to his father before Mark had disappeared, believed to be dead, Peter took personally the recent discovery of Mark Walsh's body and apparent murder. Any ill will he had for his father because of his numerous affairs and his desertion of the family didn't offset Peter's hunger for justice. Mark Walsh *was* his father, bad one though he'd been, and his murder cut too close to home for Peter to rest easily. Was the murderer's vendetta just against Mark or was there a broad conspiracy at play? Knowing that Craig, the man who'd run Walsh Enterprises for years and been like a second father to Peter, had been deliberately poisoned made the conspiracy theory more valid to Peter.

After parking in the hospital lot, Peter slammed his truck door as he headed inside.

Craig was alone in his hospital room when Peter arrived, which suited Peter just fine. He really didn't want to have the conversation he intended to have with Craig in front of his mother, who had been hovering by her lover's bedside since he'd been admitted.

"Afternoon, Craig. How's tricks?" Peter worked to keep his smile in place when he saw how pale and drawn Craig still looked even after several days of chelation therapy to rid his body of the arsenic in his system.

"Peter, good to see you. I was just about to call you." Craig rearranged the tubes that fed fluids and detoxifying agents into his blood and tried to sit up.

Seeing Craig, who'd been the picture of strength and

virility before his poisoning, laid low by the arsenic sent a chill deep into Peter's bones. *We could have lost him.*

"Looks like I saved you a call then, huh? What can I do for you?" Peter removed his coat and took a seat beside the narrow bed.

"Keep an eye on your mother for me. She's still so upset over this poisoning mess. I've told her I'm going to be fine, but you know how she worries. She's wearing herself out dividing her time between me and all her regular responsibilities with the company and her family—especially that son of yours. Her grandson is the world to her."

Guilt kicked Peter in the shins. He'd long known he depended too heavily on his mother for babysitting Patrick after school, but Jolene insisted on watching her grandson rather than hiring someone else. As a single father, Peter was grateful for the help and didn't argue the point.

"Come on, now, Craig. I thought you knew by now, no one tells Jolene Walsh to slow down. She's happiest when she's taking care of her chickadees." Peter forced a grin. He, too, had seen the strain his mother was under. Who could blame her? Having her husband's body discovered and her closest friend poisoned…

"Are you calling me a chickadee?" Craig said weakly, a smile playing at the corner of his mouth.

Peter laughed. "Never. But you know what I mean."

Craig nodded. "So what brings you around today?"

"I can't stop by to see how you're feeling?"

Sinking deeper into the stack of pillows behind him, Craig sighed. "I know you better than that, Peter. Something's on your mind, so spill."

Peter rubbed his temple and stared at his boots. "Have you heard anything else from the sheriff about who is behind your poisoning?"

"Lester Atkins is the only arrest the sheriff's made."

"Yeah, and we both know he didn't act alone. Someone paid him. Someone supplied the arsenic."

Craig nodded. "Sheriff Colton said he'd look into the possibility Atkins had help."

"Sheriff Colton is first and foremost a Colton," Peter scoffed. "I'd bet anything the Coltons had a hand in this. Maybe Damien was wrongfully convicted fifteen years ago, but I wouldn't put it past his family to have arranged my dad's *real* murder—and your poisoning—as revenge. Or to cover some other crime. Or…hell, the possibilities are endless when it comes to the Coltons."

Darius Colton and his offspring knew how to wield power and intimidate the right people. They'd been a thorn in the Walsh family's side since before Mark disappeared and Damien Colton was accused of his murder.

"I've considered the possibility that the Coltons could be involved myself. Finn's been treating me for the poisoning, so I don't think he's our man." Craig closed his eyes and sighed. "But if another Colton is responsible, how do we prove it?"

Peter gritted his teeth and shook his head. "Not through official channels, that's for sure." Because Wes Colton was the sheriff, Peter needed to find a way to circumvent the sheriff's department and get to the bottom of his father's murder and Craig's poisoning.

"I can hire someone to look into the matter. Money is no object for me." Craig paused for a breath, his weakness from the poisoning still evident. "You and your mother are family to me, and I have a feeling we haven't seen the last of these attacks. Until whoever is behind this mess is stopped, we're all still in danger. That includes you and Patrick."

A chill shimmied through Peter. Craig was right. He had to protect Patrick.

Despite his heavy case load—cheating spouses, insurance fraud, missing teenagers, adopted kids looking for their birth parents—Peter had to find the person behind the attacks.

He met Craig's dark eyes with a level stare. "I'll do the legwork myself. I have resources at my disposal, law enforcement and investigation training." *If not much time.*

He hated that taking on a private investigation into his father's death would mean more time away from Patrick. But how could he let Craig's poisoning, Mary's attack and Mark's murder go unsolved?

Craig's wan face creased with worry. "Are you sure you want to dig into your father's business and expose yourself to his skeletons?"

Peter's gut churned at the thought of the dirt he was likely to uncover on his father if he undertook this investigation of his murder. "I'm sure. But I'll need your help."

"My help?" Craig lifted the numerous IV tubes and tipped his head. "I'd love to assist you, but I'm kind of tied down at the moment."

"I need information from you. I need you to try to remember anything suspicious that may have happened at Walsh Enterprises in the weeks before my dad was murdered. Did my father contact you? Did you know he was alive?"

Craig's gaze softened. "If I'd known that, I would have told you and your brother and sisters and your mother, Peter. You know that."

"Okay." Peter waved that issue away. "Then what about the company? Any suspicious activity in the accounts or operations?"

"I'll check on that, but…my memory is a little muddled. The arsenic caused me a bit of confusion and lapses in my memory." He twitched a wry grin. "Thank God it was just poison. I thought I was getting senile."

Peter forced a grin, but reminders of how close he'd come to losing the man who'd been a surrogate father was no laughing matter. "What about threats? Had anyone contacted you—"

When Peter's cell rang, he scowled, checked the caller ID.

Honey Creek Elementary.

His pulse spiked. If the school was calling in the middle of the day, it couldn't be good news. Was Patrick sick? Hurt?

Had his father's killer come after his son?

He jabbed the talk button, his heart in his throat. "Peter Walsh."

"Hello, Mr. Walsh," a sweet female voice began. "This is Lisa Navarre. I'm Patrick's teacher."

"What's happened? Was there trouble at school?" Peter was already out of his chair and putting on his coat.

"Well, yes, there's been an incident. I need you to come to the school as soon as—"

"I'll be right there." He disconnected the call and squeezed his eyes closed. Patrick was his whole world. If anything happened to his son—

Panic rising in his throat, Peter met Craig's concerned gaze.

"Is Patrick all right?"

"I don't know. His teacher said there'd been an accident. I have to go." He backed quickly toward the door. "But we'll talk more later. I want the people responsible for doing this to you caught, Craig. I won't rest until I find everyone involved in this conspiracy."

Chapter 2

"Eyes on your own paper, Anthony." Lisa Navarre gave the student in question a firm but kind look to reiterate her directive.

Cheeks flushing, Anthony DePaulo lowered his head over his geography quiz and got back to work.

Lisa checked the clock. "Fifteen more minutes. Pace yourselves. Don't spend too much time on a question you don't—"

Her classroom door slammed open, and a tall, dark-haired man—an extremely handsome man—burst through. His eyes were wide with alarm, his manner agitated. Even before Mr. Handsome Interruption's gaze scanned the room and landed on Patrick Walsh, Lisa knew this had to be Peter Walsh. The father was the spitting image of his son. Or vice versa, she supposed. Dark brown hair roguishly in need of a trim, square-cut jaw and a generous mouth that was currently taut with concern.

"Mr. Walsh, I—"

"Patrick!" Peter Walsh rushed to his son's desk and framed his face, tipping his head as if checking for injury. "Are you all right?"

"Da-ad!" Patrick wrestled free from his father's zealous examination, while the class twittered with amusement.

"Settle down, kids. Finish your work." Lisa hustled down the row of desks to rescue Patrick from further embarrassment. "Mr. Walsh, if you would?" She tugged his arm and hitched her head toward the hall. "We can talk in the office. As you can see, the class is in the middle of a test."

Peter Walsh raised dark, bedroom eyes—okay, not bedroom eyes. He was a student's parent, so maybe that descriptor was inappropriate…but, gosh, his rich brown eyes made her belly quiver. Confusion filled his expression, then morphed to frustration or anger. Now her gut swirled for a new reason. She hated dealing with angry parents.

"Fine." Mr. Walsh gave one last glance to his son before stalking out to the hallway.

"Keep working, kids. I'll be right back." Lisa swept her practiced be-on-your-best-behavior look around the room, meeting the eyes of several of her more…er, *loquacious* students before she joined Mr. Walsh in the corridor.

He launched into her before she could open her mouth. "What's going on? You called me here because there'd been—"

"Mr. Walsh." Lisa held up a hand to cut him off, then caught the attention of the school librarian who was walking past them. "Ms. Fillmore, would you mind sitting with my class for a few minutes while I talk with Mr. Walsh in the office?"

"Certainly," the older woman said with a smile.

"They're taking a geography quiz. You'll need to pick up the papers at exactly two-thirty if I'm not back."

"Got it. Two-thirty." Ms. Fillmore gave a little wave as she disappeared into the classroom.

When Lisa turned back to Patrick's father, she met a glare that would freeze a volcano. "You lied to me. You said Patrick had been in an accident. Do you have any idea how worried I was on the way over here?"

Patience. Keep your cool. Let him vent if he needs to.

Drawing a deep breath to collect herself, she flashed him a warm smile. "Let's go to the office where we can speak privately." She motioned down the hall and started toward the front of the school. When Mr. Walsh only stared at her stubbornly for a moment, she paused to wait for him to follow. Handsome or not, the man clearly had a temper when it came to his son.

Lisa could understand that. Most parents had an emotional hot button when it came to their children. Sweet, soft-spoken members of the quilting club became growling mama bears when they thought their cubs needed protecting or defending.

Finally, Peter Walsh fell in step behind her, his long-legged strides quickly catching up with hers. "Why did you tell me there'd been an accident?"

"I didn't," she returned calmly.

"You di—"

"I said *incident*. With an *i*. You hung up before I could explain the nature of the problem."

Mr. Walsh drew a breath as if to mount an argument, then snapped his mouth closed. His brow creased, and his jaw tightened as if replaying their brief phone conversation and realizing his mistake.

"I'm sorry if I alarmed you. Patrick is fine, physically."

They reached the front office, and Lisa escorted him into a vacant conference room. "Please, have a seat."

Patrick's father crossed his arms over his chest and narrowed a suspicious gaze on her. "Thanks, I'll stand."

Okay. She faced him, squaring her shoulders and staring at his forehead…because looking into those dark eyes was just too distracting. Too unnerving.

Darn it all, she was a professional. She couldn't let this man rattle her.

"Mr. Walsh, I called you because Patrick was disrupting class today and—"

"Disrupting how?" he interrupted, his back stiffening.

"He burped."

Mr. Walsh's eyebrows snapped together in confusion. "Excuse me? He burped?"

"Yes."

He shifted his weight and angled an irritated look toward her. "You called me down here to tell me he *burped?*" His angry tone and volume rose. "Kids will burp sometimes, lady. It's a fact of life. Maybe you should be talking to the lunch ladies about the food they're serving instead of calling parents away from important business to report their kids' bodily functions, for crying out loud!"

Patience. Lisa balled then flexed her fingers, struggling to keep her cool. She made the mistake of meeting his eyes then, and her stomach flip-flopped. Good grief, the man had sexy eyes!

"It wasn't just a small, my-lunch-didn't-sit-right burp, Mr. Walsh. It was loud. Forced. Designed to get a rise out of his classmates."

Peter Walsh rocked back on his boot heels, listening. At least, she hoped he was listening. Some parents wore blinders when it came to their kids' behavior. Their little darling couldn't possibly have done the things she said.

Lisa took a slow calming breath, working to keep her voice even and non-confrontational.

"He'd been disruptive all morning—talking, getting out of his seat without permission, making rude noises, even poking the girl in front of him for no apparent reason. The loud belching was just the final straw."

Peter Walsh had the nerve to roll his eyes and shake his head. Lisa gritted her teeth.

"With all due respect, Ms. Navaro—" he started in a tone that was far from respectful.

"It's *Navarre*, Mr. Walsh."

"Navarre," he repeated, lifting his hand in concession, but his disposition remained hard and challenging. "It seems to me keeping order in your classroom is *your* job. Send him to the principal's office if you need to, but don't drag me down here every time my son acts up in class… or *burps*. You shouldn't have to call a kid's parent away from their job to handle a minor behavior problem. If you can't keep a ten-year-old boy in line for a few hours a day, perhaps you're in the wrong profession."

Lisa's hackles went up. She'd already wondered if teaching children was the best place for her, but for reasons that had nothing to do with her ability to discipline her class. She suppressed the ache that nudged her heart and focused on the matter at hand.

"I'm perfectly capable of maintaining order in my classroom, Mr. Walsh." She drilled him with a look that her students knew well, the one that said she'd reached the limits of her patience. "Especially if I have the cooperation of the children's parents in addressing at home any issues that may be at the root of behavior problems."

He scoffed. "My son does not have a behavior problem. He may be having a bad day today, but you know as well as I do that he's not a troublemaker."

"Which, if you'd let me finish explaining, is why I called you to come down for a conference. Usually Patrick is quite well-behaved. In fact, since the beginning of school, it seems he's become more quiet, even withdrawn. His grades have slipped in recent weeks. Did you know that? I've sent home his test papers to be signed, but you never sign them. His grandmother does."

"My mother babysits him most afternoons until I can get home from work. My job keeps me on the road a lot, and I've had to work longer hours lately, so Patrick's grandmother handles his schoolwork."

"But you're his parent, Mr. Walsh. You need to be involved."

His face darkened, and he narrowed a glare on her. "Are you telling me how to parent my kid?"

Why not? You were just trying to tell me how to do my job! Lisa bit back the caustic retort that would serve no purpose other than make her feel better for five minutes. Then she'd feel bad that she'd lost her temper and kick herself for being reactionary.

"No, sir. I'm not." She purposefully infused her tone with calm and concern, enough to capture the agitated father's attention. She had to be sure he heard and understood the importance of her next statement. "But earlier today, when I warned Patrick that I would have to call you if he didn't behave, his response was, 'Go ahead. Call my dad. He won't care. He's too busy to care about what I do.'"

Peter Walsh jerked back as if slapped, his expression stunned. "That's…crazy! He knows I care about him. He knows I *love* him! More than anything in this world."

"Maybe up here he knows that." She tapped her head. "But kids need to see that love and affection in action to reaffirm what you say. He needs to see you express interest in his schoolwork, in his friends, in his life to really believe it here." She moved her hand to her heart.

A muscle in his jaw twitched, and he shifted his glowering gaze to a bulletin board on the far wall. "The last few months have been...especially difficult for my family, Ms. Navarre. I've tried to protect Patrick from most of the fallout, shield him from the worst of it, but..." He heaved a sigh and left his sentence unfinished.

"I read the newspaper. I know about your father's murder, and I'm terribly sorry for your loss."

His eyes snapped to hers. Pain shadowed his gaze, and her heart went out to him. She'd seen a similar sadness in Patrick's eyes too many times since the school year had started. "The reason I called you here is not because Patrick was acting out. I can handle disciplining students when it is called for."

Chagrin flickered across his face, and he shifted his weight.

"I called because I'm worried about Patrick. I think the recent events in your family have upset him, and he doesn't feel he can talk to you about it. He feels alone because he thinks you're too busy for him. He's confused and scared."

Worry lined Peter Walsh's face. "He said that?"

"His withdrawal said that. His grades said that. His misbehavior today said that. I've been a teacher for six years. I've seen this before. He just needs reassurance from you that his world is safe, that you care, that he is your priority. Mr. Walsh, more than discipline, what Patrick needs is his father."

Peter squared his shoulders, a bit of his temper returning. Obviously, he took her last comment as an indictment. "I'll talk to him tonight. You won't have problems with his behavior again."

Lisa's heart sank. Had he heard her at all?

Peter Walsh, his square jaw tight and his back stiff, turned to stalk out of the conference room.

"Mr. Walsh, I—"

But he was gone. All six feet plus of seething testosterone and brooding eyes. Lisa inhaled deeply, hoping to calm her frazzled nerves, but instead drew in the enticing scents of leather and pine that Peter Walsh left in his wake.

She had no business thinking of her student's father in the terms that filtered through her head—sexy, virile—but with a man like Peter Walsh, how could she not?

Lisa dropped into a chair and raked fingers through her raven hair. She needed to collect herself before she returned to her class.

But five minutes later, as she headed back to her room, her mind was still full of Peter Walsh and his smoldering dark eyes.

Patrick tossed his backpack on the floor of Peter's truck and gave his father a forlorn glance as he climbed onto the seat. "So I guess I'm in big trouble, huh?"

Peter shrugged. "Depends on what you call big trouble. I understand you gave your teacher a good bit of grief today. You were loud and disruptive in class. You know better than that, sport."

"Am I grounded?"

"Do you think you should be grounded?"

Patrick hesitated, got a scheming glint in his eyes. "No? I think I've learned my lesson, and we can skip the punishment?" He lifted hopeful dark eyes to his father.

"Seriously? I think I hear a question mark in your answer. You know I can't just let this slide. What if I'd been working a big case out of town when I got called to the school? Huh?"

Patrick scowled. "You're always working big cases out of town. Why can't you have a regular job like everyone else?"

Peter's chest tightened. He'd heard Patrick complain about his work hours before, but in light of his teacher's concerns, Peter took his son's comments more seriously this time. "Patrick, you know I'd spend more time with you if I could. There's nothing in the world more important to me than you are, but I have to earn a living and pay our bills. My job demands that I be gone a lot. I can't change that."

But even as he said as much, a niggling voice in his head argued the point. He *could* rearrange his schedule or be more selective in the cases he took on so that he could have more time at home with Patrick. Even if the more lucrative cases took him out of town, couldn't they tighten their monetary belts a bit in order for him to be more attentive to his son's needs?

He glanced over at Patrick's long face, slumped shoulders. Guilt pricked Peter.

"Tell you what—I'll make a special effort to cut back on my hours and do more stuff with you—"

Immediately, Patrick's eyes brightened, and he snapped an eager gaze up to his father's.

"If—"

Patrick rolled his eyes and groaned. "I knew there was a catch."

Peter shot his son a stern glance. "Don't interrupt. You have to promise me you'll work hard at bringing your grades up. Mrs. Navarre said your work has been slipping."

"*Ms.* Navarre, Dad. She's not married."

Peter quirked an eyebrow, mentally flashing to when he'd been corrected by the woman herself on the pronunciation of her name. He worked to school his expression and hide his intrigue with this new tidbit of information. He'd been too worked up, too worried about Patrick during his altercation with the attractive brunette to look for a ring. But even as upset as he'd been, he hadn't missed Ms. Navarre's shapely curves or model-worthy face.

Hell, he couldn't blame Patrick for being distracted and having faltering grades with a teacher as hot as Lisa Navarre. Any male over the age of nine would be distracted by Patrick's teacher.

Peter squeezed the steering wheel and cleared his throat. "Ms. Navarre also said that you were talking back to her, being rude." Peter cast a disapproving look to his son. "Burping."

Patrick chuckled. "Yeah, it was a good one, too, Dad. Really low and loud and—"

"Patrick," Peter said, a warning clear in his tone. "It was rude and inappropriate."

"But Da-ad—"

Peter raised a hand, anticipating the coming argument. "I know that we sometimes goof around at home and do stuff like that, but…there's a time and a place for that kind of behavior and school is *not* the time or place."

God, when had he started sounding like his father? No. Not his father. More like his *mother*. Egad. *That* was scary. Peter cringed internally.

But Mark Walsh had never been interested in teaching his son wrong and right. He'd been too busy cheating on his wife. Acid burned in Peter's belly at the memory, and he swore to himself, again, that he'd be a better father to Patrick than Mark Walsh had been to him.

Mr. Walsh, more than discipline, what Patrick needs is his father.

"Patrick, I think the thing I find most disturbing about what happened at school today is that you sassed your teacher. I didn't raise you to·disrespect adults and especially not a lady."

"That's no lady, that's my teacher," Patrick said in a deep voice, mimicking the comedian they'd watched on television together the past weekend.

Peter had to bite the inside of his cheek so that he wouldn't laugh. He couldn't encourage Patrick's misbehavior, even if he did find his son's sense of humor amusing.

Instead, he gave Patrick the look all parents have instinctively. The I-mean-business-and-you're-treading-on-thin-ice look.

"Tomorrow, first thing when you get to school, you will apologize to Ms. Navarre for being rude and disruptive."

Patrick gave a dramatic sigh and stared out the window.

"Look at me." When he had his son's attention he added, "And you're grounded for…" Peter did a quick calculation. What length of punishment suited the crime? And why *wasn't* there an instruction manual for parents? Raising his son alone was, hands-down, the hardest thing he'd ever done.

And the most rewarding, he thought as he held his boy's dark gaze. "For the weekend. No video games, no TV, no going to your friends'."

"What!" Patrick grunted. "What's left?"

"Try reading a book, or catching up on your schoolwork. Or…going fishing with me."

"Hello? Dad…it's November. It's freezing."

"What, you don't think fish get hungry in November?" He tugged up the corner of his mouth. "Okay, so…we'll save fishing for spring, and we'll…" Peter turned up his palm as he thought. "Catch a football game together."

"You said no TV."

"I know. I'm talking about going *to* a game. Live. I bet

I can still get us tickets to see the Bobcats play. What do ya think?"

Patrick's face lit with enthusiasm. "Montana State? Seriously, Dad? Can we?" Patrick whooped.

"I'll take that as a yes," Peter chuckled as his son bounced in his seat. "But remember our deal."

Patrick screwed up his face. "What deal?"

Peter shook his head in frustration. "You're going to bring up your grades, apologize to your teacher and promise me that your days of clowning around in class are over. Got it, buddy?"

Patrick slumped back against the seat, a contrite expression pulling his mouth taut. "Yes, sir."

On the way home from school, Lisa stopped at Salon Allegra for a pedicure. Sure, it was November and no one except her would likely see her bare feet until next spring, but after standing all day and dealing with Patrick Walsh's aggravated father, she figured she deserved a little pampering. Heck, she might get a manicure, too.

Lisa pulled the collar of her parka up around her chin as she bustled into the beauty shop. The bell over the front door tinkled as she entered, announcing her arrival to the staff. The shop's owner, Eve Kelley, looked up from the appointment book at the front desk and sent her a bright smile.

"Afternoon, Lisa. What brings you in on this blustery day?" Eve's blue eyes shone warmly, her girl-next-door-meets-cheerleader friendliness in place as always.

"Hi, Eve. I need a pick-me-up in the worst way. I thought I'd get a pedicure if you could work me in."

"Well…" Eve glanced to her beauticians, each with a customer already, and gnawed her bottom lip.

"If you're too busy, I'll—"

"Nonsense. I'll get you fixed up myself." She picked up a tube of salted crackers and motioned for Lisa to follow. "So...bad day at school?"

"Not for the most part. Plans for the rescheduled fall festival are going well. But one of my better students decided to act out today, and when I called his father in for a conference, I got an earful. Dad settled down a little once I got the chance to explain myself, but...whew! Confrontations with parents always leave me wrung out."

"I bet." Eve patted an elevated chair, showing Lisa where to sit, and set her crackers on a nearby table. As Eve took her seat, Lisa noticed the former prom queen and cheerleader had unbuttoned her jeans at the waist, as if they didn't quite fit anymore.

Had Eve put on a couple of pounds? Lisa couldn't really tell.

The beauty shop owner look as gorgeous as ever to her. Eve turned and caught Lisa staring, speculating. "So who was this irate father?"

"Oh, uh...Peter Walsh."

Eve paused in her preparations for Lisa's pedicure. "Peter Walsh? But Peter's always struck me as the laid-back, easygoing sort." Eve flashed her a devilish grin and wiggled her eyebrows. "The *extremely hot,* laid-back, easygoing sort."

An image of Peter Walsh's broad shoulders and rough-hewn jawline taunted her as Lisa returned a smile. "Oh, he is good-looking, no lie. But when it comes to his son, he apparently has a bit of pit bull in him."

"Hmm." Eve hummed as she nibbled a cracker and tipped her head in thought. "I've known the Walsh family for years. Peter has never been overly social, but also never anything but kind and polite. He's had a tough road, raising Patrick on his own."

When Eve paused to munch another cracker, Lisa asked, "What happened to Patrick's mother?"

A shadow crossed Eve's face, her sculpted eyebrows puckering with some dark emotion. "She died...in childbirth." Eve's gaze drifted away, across the room, as she recalled the details. She rubbed a hand over her belly almost without thought.

An odd tingle of recognition nipped Lisa's nape. She glanced at Eve's crackers then studied the pretty blonde's glowing face. Could she be...?

"Katie and Peter were so young," Eve said and shook her head sorrowfully. "Probably only nineteen or so, but they'd been high-school sweethearts and married right after graduation. Katie's death crushed Peter. And after losing his father a few years earlier...well, we *thought* his dad was dead..."

Eve gave her head a shake and puffed out a breath. "But that's a whole other can of worms. One more freak tragedy for him and his family to have to deal with." Jamming one more cracker in her mouth, Eve turned on the jets of the steaming foot bath for Lisa to soak in.

Lisa slipped off her shoes and socks, giving her sore feet a little rub before sinking them in the warm water. Her fatigue now pressed on her with a more somber note, but she couldn't blame Peter Walsh for her gray mood.

Mention of childbirth gone wrong and the subtle clues that Eve was pregnant stirred up painful memories. Memories that were better locked away where they couldn't haunt her.

Shoving down thoughts of the baby she'd never have, Lisa wiggled her toes in the steaming foot bath and redirected her thoughts to the subject at hand. "So Peter has raised Patrick alone since his birth?"

"Yep. Although I'm sure his family gives him plenty of help and babysitting services. Jolene can't say enough glowing things about Patrick when she's in here." Eve smiled wistfully. "Like any good grandma would." She started working on Lisa's right foot, buffing, trimming and shaping. "Anyway… don't let this first impression of Peter Walsh color your opinion of him. He really is a great guy. Any gal would be lucky to have him."

"Whoa!" Lisa held up her hands. "I never said anything about dating him. I'm not looking for a husband."

Eve flipped her blond hair over her shoulder and flashed Lisa a saucy look. "Who said anything about *you?* He might be ten years younger than me but…hoo-baby! When a guy looks that good, who cares about age?"

They both laughed, and Lisa felt a little of her tension melt away.

"So what color on the toes?" Eve asked, pulling out a large tray of nail polish.

"Oh, just a basic pink or mauve is fine."

Eve scrunched up her nose. "Pink is so boring, girlfriend. How about this new sexy red I got in last week? Or…oh, I know! Electric purple!"

Lisa snorted. "Me? Purple?"

Eve wiggled the bottle and raised her eyebrows with enthusiasm. "Come on. Be daring! It looks really sexy."

Lisa shrugged. "What the heck. Paint me purple. Not like anyone but my cat is gonna see my toes anyway."

And thanks to her inability to have children, Lisa thought with a pang of sorrow, that was how things were likely to be for a long time. Even her attempt to adopt once had ended in heartache.

No children. No husband. No family.

A lonely ache settled over her. Her infertility hadn't just robbed her of a child, but also the future she craved.

Peter flipped his wrist to check the time. "Better get a move on, sport. School bus will be here any minute."

"Do you gotta work out of town again today?" Patrick asked around a mouthful of cereal.

"Nope. I wrapped up the legwork on a case yesterday, so I'll mostly be working from home today to get the paperwork finished. Why?"

His son shrugged. "Just wonderin' if you'd be here when I got home or if Grandma would."

He feels alone, because he thinks you're too busy for him.

Lisa Navarre's assessment rang in Peter's head, and he studied the droop in Patrick's shoulders as he slurped sugary milk from his breakfast bowl.

"I'll make a point of being here when you get off the bus today. Okay, sport? After you do your homework, we'll do something together. Your choice."

Patrick gave him a withering look that said parents were the stupidest creatures on earth. "Dad, it's Friday. I don't have homework on Fridays."

"Good," Peter returned with good humor. "Then we'll have more time to do something together."

"Can we play on the Wii?"

Peter was about to agree when he remembered yesterday's punishment. "Aren't you grounded for the weekend?"

Patrick's face fell. "Oh, yeah."

Outside, the bus tooted its horn.

"Time's up. Grab your backpack!" Peter hurried to the front door to wave to the bus driver, while Patrick struggled out. "Don't worry. We'll find something fun to do that doesn't include the TV. And… I haven't forgotten about taking you to see the football game tomorrow."

Patrick's face brightened as he rushed past. "Cool. Bye, Dad!"

"Don't forget to apologize to Ms. Navarre!"

His son gave a wave as he climbed on the bus, and Peter sighed. Patrick wasn't the only one who owed the attractive brunette an apology. He'd been pretty hostile, when Patrick's teacher had only had his son's best interests at heart.

Peter scrubbed a hand over his unshaven cheeks as he went back in his house. His only lame excuse for his shameful behavior was that he'd already been pumped full of adrenaline after the brush with Bill Rigsby's shotgun-toting neighbor, and he'd been spoiling for a fight after his meeting with Craig, where the Coltons, his least-favorite family, had been high on the list of suspects. But he should never have let his bad mood taint his treatment of Patrick's teacher.

Peter took Patrick's half-eaten cereal to the sink and ate a few bites himself before dumping the rest.

Jamming his thumbs in his jeans pockets, he headed into the den where he had his PC set up in one corner. Perhaps on Monday, he'd drive Patrick to school and make a point of speaking to Ms. Navarre. His pulse spiked a notch, a bump that had more to do with his anticipation of seeing Patrick's teacher again than his morning caffeine kicking in. He thumbed the power button on the computer and leaned back in his chair as the monitor hummed to life.

In the face of his shouting and sarcasm, Lisa Navarre had not only held her own, but she'd kept her tone calm and her arguments constructive and focused on Patrick's needs. He respected her for her professionalism and grace under fire.

And the fact Lisa Navarre had sexy curves and a spark of stubborn courage in her dark eyes only made her more intriguing to Peter. Knowing her observations of Patrick in the classroom mirrored his own suspicions about Patrick's difficulty processing the most recent family troubles gave him reason to call on her expertise. Perhaps the attractive teacher would give him a bit of her time and help him figure out the best way to handle the recent family crises with Patrick.

When his computer finished loading the start-up programs, Peter opened his case file on Bill Rigsby and got to work, but his mind drifted again to the same family issues that had had him distracted yesterday on his stakeout. His visit with Craig at the hospital only confirmed that someone outside the Colton family needed to be looking into his father's murder and who'd paid Atkins to poison Craig.

Peter lifted his coffee mug and squeezed the handle until his knuckles blanched. How could Sheriff Wes Colton possibly conduct an unbiased investigation when his own family was most likely at fault? What secrets and evidence was Wes suppressing to protect his brood of vipers? Craig may have ruled out Finn, since Finn was his doctor, but Peter wasn't willing to make that leap of faith yet.

Peter gritted his teeth and shoved away from the computer. Enough waiting for answers. He'd go down to the sheriff's office and demand answers from Wes Colton.

Even if Mark Walsh had been a half-hearted father and a two-timing husband, he deserved justice. And Craig Warner, the man who'd managed the reins at Walsh Enterprises for almost two decades and who'd been a father figure to Peter, deserved answers about who'd poisoned him.

Peter refused to rest until he had the truth.

* * *

As Peter strode up the front walk to the county courthouse, he huddled deeper into the warmth of his suede coat. A chill November wind announced the approach of another bitterly cold Montana winter, a bleak time of year that reflected Peter's current mood. He glanced up to the steepled clock tower in the red brick and natural stone edifice where the sheriff's office had told him he could find Wes Colton that morning, waiting to testify in a court hearing. The woman at the sheriff's office had said she thought Wes was due at the courthouse by 9:00 a.m.

But if he wasn't, Peter would wait.

He nodded a good-morning to an elderly man who shuffled out the front door of the courthouse, then shucked his gloves as he entered the lobby and got his bearings. The scents of freshly brewed coffee, floor cleaner and age filled the halls of the old building. Peter could remember thinking how old the courthouse seemed when he'd come down here with his mother to get his driver's license when he was sixteen. Little about the building had changed in the intervening years, even if Peter felt he'd lived a lifetime since then.

Jamming his gloves in his coat pocket, Peter spotted Wes Colton down a long corridor and headed purposefully towards him. "Sheriff?"

Wes turned, lifting his eyes from the foam cup of coffee he sipped. The sheriff stilled, his expression growing wary, before he lowered his cup and squared his shoulders, taking a defensive stance.

"Peter." Wes gave a terse nod of greeting. "Something I can do for you?"

"Yeah. You can tell me why no one's been arrested yet for my father's murder." Peter stood with his arms akimbo, his chin jutted forward.

A muscle in Wes's jaw tightened as the sheriff ground his back teeth. "Because we don't have enough evidence to make an arrest stick yet."

"You've had more than four months. What the hell's taking so long?"

"We're doing all we can." The sheriff lifted one eyebrow, his blue eyes as cold as his tone. "I'm sure you wouldn't want us hauling anyone in prematurely, just to lose an indictment due to lack of good evidence." Wes paused and canted his head to the side, his eyes narrowing. "Unlike the last time your father was *murdered,* I intend to build a case based on solid evidence. Forensics. Facts. Not the circumstantial tripe and suspicion they used to railroad my brother when your father pulled his disappearing act years ago."

Peter stiffened. He should have known this discussion would deteriorate to a rehashing of the Walsh and Colton families' ancient feud. Even before Mark Walsh had forbidden his eldest daughter, Lucy, to date Damien Colton, the families had been rivals. Two powerful families in the same small town couldn't help but butt heads every now and then, in business, or in politics, or, in the case of Lucy and Damien, in the personal lives of their children.

"Your brother may have been innocent of murder, but even your family can't deny he looked guilty as sin."

Wes curled his lip in a sneer. "Thanks to your family greasing the skids of the judicial system to see that the prosecutor's flimsy circumstantial case slid by the judges and jury."

Peter stepped closer, aiming a finger at Wes's chest. "We did no such thing!"

The sheriff sent a pointed gaze to Peter's finger before meeting his eyes again. "Want to back off before I charge you with assaulting an officer?"

Drawing a deep breath, Peter dropped his hand to his side, balling his fingers into a fist. "Just tell me where the current case stands. Who are you investigating? What clues do you have?"

Wes shrugged casually. "Everyone's a suspect until the investigation is closed."

"Don't give me that crap. I want answers, Colton!" Damn, but the Coltons could push Peter's buttons.

He paused only long enough to force his tone and volume down a notch. A public brawl with the sheriff would serve no purpose other than to land him in jail for disorderly conduct. "What are you doing to catch my father's murderer?"

"I'm not at liberty to discuss an ongoing investigation."

When Peter shifted his weight, ready to launch into another attack, another round of questions, Wes lifted a hand to forestall any arguments. "And I'm not just saying that to get you off my back or because there's no love lost between our families. I truly can't answer any question for you right now."

"That's not good enough."

"It has to be."

Peter clenched his teeth. "I have a right to know who killed my father."

"And you will. As soon as I know." The sheriff pinned a hard look on Peter. "But I won't blow this case by tipping my hand prematurely or letting you or anyone else pressure me into making an arrest for the sake of making an arrest. My brother knows all too well what happens when vigilante justice is served rather than reason and law. My deputies and I are conducting a thorough investigation. We'll find the person responsible. Don't doubt that."

Scoffing, Peter shook his head. "Well, forgive me if I

don't take you on your word, Sheriff *Colton*. I haven't seen any progress on the case in weeks, and now Craig Warner's been poisoned, too."

"And you think the two incidents are connected." A statement, not a question.

"Damn straight. And I'd hardly call my father's murder and the attempted murder of a family friend 'incidents.' They're felonies. Need I remind you that someone ran Mary off the road a couple months ago? How do we know that whoever is responsible won't come after someone else in my family?"

"We don't."

The sheriff's flat, frank response punched Peter in the gut. When he recovered the wherewithal to speak, he scowled darkly at Wes. "And that doesn't bother you, Sheriff? You may not like me or my family, but I have a ten-year-old son at home. How are you going to feel if he gets hurt because you didn't do your job and find the scumbag who killed my father?"

Wes hooked his thumbs in his pockets and rolled his shoulders. "Believe it or not, I'd feel terrible—and not because I didn't do my job, because I am doing everything humanly possible to catch the bastard. No, because I'm not the inept, hard-hearted fool you seem to think I am. I don't want to see anyone else hurt. But I have to work within the law. A proper investigation takes time. There are forces at work behind the scenes that you may not see, but which are busy 24/7 looking at this case from every angle."

Peter gritted his teeth, completely unsatisfied with the runaround and placating assurances he was getting from the sheriff. "Here's an angle you may have missed. Not only do I think Craig Warner's poisoning is related to my father's murder, I think your family is involved. I'd bet my life a Colton is behind everything."

Wes's glare was glacial. "Do you have any proof to back up that accusation?"

"Not yet. But I can get it."

The sheriff's eyes narrowed even further. "I'm warning you, Walsh. Don't interfere with my investigation. If you so much as stick a toe over the line, I'll throw the book at you."

Peter pulled his gloves from his pocket, signaling an end to the conversation. "I would expect as much."

Chapter 3

Thanks to a new missing-person case on Friday and his promise to take Patrick to the game on Saturday, Sunday afternoon was the first chance Peter had to follow up on his suspicions regarding the Colton family's connection to Craig's poisoning and his father's murder. The best place to start, Peter always figured, was the beginning—in this case, the circumstances and events surrounding the Coltons at the time of Mark Walsh's first "death" in 1995.

He left Patrick in the capable hands of his mother, Jolene, and headed to the library to begin his research. In 1995, when his father went missing and was presumed dead, Peter had been a typically self-absorbed teenager. He hadn't cared what political causes or social events his family or the rival Coltons were involved in. But in hindsight, he thought maybe he could glean some helpful information to focus his investigation.

As he headed into the library from the parking lot, he

noticed a number of large limbs and debris still cluttered the lawn. He frowned at the reminders of the tornado that had struck Honey Creek recently. Most of the brick and stone buildings in town had survived with minimal or no damage, but many homes, including his own, had sustained varying degrees of damage. He scanned the library's brick exterior searching for signs of damage before mounting the steps to enter the front door.

He spotted his younger sister, Mary, near the front desk and made a beeline toward her. "Well, if it isn't the future Mrs. Jake Pierson."

Mary's head snapped up, and a broad smile filled her face. "Peter! How are you?"

Love—and Mary's recent, significant weight loss— looked good on his sister. She positively glowed with her newfound happiness.

"Clearly not as well as you. Look at that radiant flush in your face." He tweaked his sister's cheek playfully, and she swatted his hand away. "So what are you doing here? I thought your days as librarian were over now that you and Jake are opening the security biz."

She leaned a hip against the front desk and grinned. "I may not work here, but I have friends who do. And I volunteer to lead the story time in the children's area on Sunday afternoons. What brings *you* in today, and why didn't you bring my favorite nephew with you?"

"Mom's watching Patrick so I can get some research done." Peter unbuttoned his coat and glanced around at the tables where people were scattered, reading and studying. An attractive dark-haired woman at one of the corner tables snagged his attention.

Lisa Navarre.

Patrick's teacher was hunched over thick books, scribbling in a notebook and looking for all the world like a college co-ed the night before exams. Her rich chocolate hair was pinned up haphazardly, wisps falling around her face. A pencil rested above her ear, and a pair of frameless reading glasses slid down her nose. Chewing the cap of her pen, she looked adorably geeky and maddeningly sexy at the same time.

Peter stared openly, his pulse revving, and his conscience tickling. No time like the present to apologize for his oafish behavior on Thursday afternoon.

"Hello? Peter?" Mary waved a hand in front of him and laughed as he snapped back to attention. "I asked what kind of research you were doing. Geez, bro, where did you go just then?"

Peter shifted awkwardly, embarrassed at being caught staring. "Sorry. I saw someone I need to talk to."

Mary glanced the direction he'd been looking. "Would that someone be an attractive single female who teaches at the elementary school?"

Peter ignored the question and his sister's knowing grin. "Say, where do they keep the microfiche around here? I need to look through old issues of the *Honey Creek Gazette*."

Mary shifted through a stack of children's books, setting some aside and discarding others. She thumbed through the pages of a colorful picture book, then added it to her growing stack.

He tipped his head and smirked. "Just how many books are you planning on reading to the story-time kids?"

Pausing, she looked at the tall pile. "Looks like about fifteen to me. But I could always add more later." She gave him a smug grin. "How far back do you want to go with the *Gazette?* Anything older than two years is filed in a room at the back. Lily will have to get it for you."

When she nodded toward the other end of the check-out

desk, Peter shifted his attention to the raven-haired woman who'd earned a bad reputation before leaving town years ago. Now Lily Masterson was back in town, repairing her reputation after being hired as the head librarian. She was also Wes Colton's fiancée.

Tensing, Peter took Mary by the elbow and led her several steps away from the front desk. "I want everything from 1995."

Mary stilled and cast him a suspicious look. Clearly she recognized the time frame as when their father disappeared. "What are you doing, Peter?"

He rubbed the back of his neck and sighed. "Looking for the answers that the sheriff either refuses to find himself or is covering up to protect his family."

Mary's shoulders drooped, and she lowered her voice. "You make it sound like Dad's disappearance was part of a big conspiracy with the Coltons."

He twitched a shoulder. "Maybe it was."

She looked skeptical. "Look, Peter, I don't know what you're up to, but be careful. When Jake and I dug into Dad's death this summer, we clearly rattled some skeletons. This research you're here for could lead to trouble for you if word gets out. I don't want to see you or Patrick in any danger."

Craig had said as much, too, when he'd visited him in the hospital. Peter's gut rolled at the suggestion his investigation could threaten Patrick's safety.

"And considering that Damien was proven innocent of killing dad, since dad wasn't really dead all these years," Mary added, "I'm not sure what sort of conspiracy you think the Coltons are involved in. But Jake trusts Wes, and that's good enough for me. What makes you think Wes isn't doing his job?"

Peter glanced around the bustling library, his gaze

stopping on Lily. "That's a conversation for another day and another, more private place." He shoved his hands deep in his jeans pockets. "So do you still have access to the *Gazette* microfiche? I really don't want the sheriff's new girlfriend knowing I'm digging into his family's history."

She frowned and flipped her red hair over her shoulder. "I can't access the back room anymore, but I'll ask Lily to get the microfiche you need. Meet me over by the film reader." She jerked her head in the general direction of the microfiche machine on a far wall, then headed across the room to speak to Lily.

Peter noted the machine she indicated but headed the opposite direction. He had to eat a bit of humble pie.

Wiping his suddenly perspiring palms on the seat of his jeans, Peter headed toward the table where Lisa Navarre sat. As he approached, she paused from her work long enough to stretch the kinks from her back and roll her shoulders. When her gaze landed on him, he saw recognition tinged with surprise register on her face, along with another emotion he couldn't identify. She seemed uneasy or flustered somehow as he stepped up to her table and flashed her an awkward grin. He couldn't really blame her for being disconcerted by his presence. He'd been rather gruff and unpleasant last time they met.

Ms. Navarre snatched off her reading glasses and smoothed a hand over her untidy hair. "Mr. Walsh… hello."

He rocked back on his heels and hooked his thumbs in his front pockets. "Hi, Ms. Navarre. I'm sorry to interrupt. Do you have a minute?"

She closed the massive book in front of her and waved a dismissive hand over her notepad. "Sure. I was just doing a little studying for my class."

Peter read the title of the book. "*Critical Evaluation in*

Higher Education. Huh, I didn't know fourth grade was considered higher education nowadays."

She tucked one of the stray wisps of hair behind her ear and sent him a quick grin. "It's not for Patrick's class. I'm working on my PhD in Higher Education. I'm thinking of moving to teaching college-level classes instead of elementary."

"Because at the college level you won't have to deal with jerk fathers who read you the riot act for doing your job?" He added a crooked smile and earned a half grin in return.

"Well, there is that." Her expression brightened. "Although, for the record, the term *jerk* is yours, not mine. *Concerned, somewhat overwrought fathers* might be a better term."

"Call it what you want, but I still acted like a jerk." He met her golden-brown eyes and his chest tightened. "Please forgive me for taking you to task. I do appreciate your concern for Patrick and your willingness to bring his errant behavior that day to my attention. I'd already had a rather stressful day and was on edge about some family matters, but that's no excuse for the way I bit your head off."

She blinked and set her glasses aside. "Wow. That's, um… Apology accepted. Thank you."

Peter noticed a pink tint staining her cheeks and added her ability to blush to the growing list of things he liked about Patrick's teacher. "So if jerk fathers aren't why you're thinking of moving up to higher education, what *is* behind the career change?"

"Well…" Her dark eyebrows knitted, and she fumbled with her pen. "My reasons will sound really bad without knowing the whole long, boring personal story behind my decision. Let's just say teaching older students would be less…painful." She winced. "Ooo, that sounded more melodramatic than I intended." She laughed awkwardly and waved her hand as if to erase her last comment. "Forget I said that."

"Forgotten." But Peter had already filed both the comment and the shadow that flitted across her face in his memory bank. He had no business delving deeper into her personal life, but he couldn't deny he was intrigued. And sympathetic to her discomfort. He had painful things in his past that he avoided discussing when possible.

"Is Patrick with you?" she asked looking past him toward the children's section.

"No. Not today. I'm here on business matters, looking for information for a case I'm working on."

He could tell by the wrinkle in her brow that his working on the weekend away from Patrick bothered her. A jab of guilt prodded him to add, "But yesterday, Patrick and I took in the MSU game and spent most of the evening playing Monopoly together."

"Oh, good." Her lips curved, although the smile didn't reach her eyes. "I'm sure he enjoyed that."

"I hope so. You made some valid points the other day at school."

She blinked as if surprised, and Peter chuckled. "Despite how it may have seemed, I was listening. I heard what you said about Patrick's withdrawal and falling grades."

She held up a finger. "Um, *slipping.* I believe I said his grades were slipping."

He scratched his chin. "The difference being…?"

"His grades are still good. They've come down a bit, just a few points. But *falling* to me is more dramatic. Big drop, by several letter grades."

Peter chuckled. "You are a master of nuance, aren't you? *Incident* not *accident. Slipping* not *falling.*"

She flushed a deeper shade of pink, and Peter's libido gave him another hard kick.

"I'm not trying to be difficult. I just believe in saying what I mean. Exactly what I mean."

Mary caught his attention from across the room. With an impatient look, she held up the microfiche Lily had retrieved for her.

"Well, I don't want to keep you from your studying." Peter motioned to her books then took a step back. "I just wanted you to know I'm sorry for shouting at you."

"Thank you, Mr. Walsh." She held out her hand, and he grasped her fingers. Her handshake was firm and confident, and the feel of her warm hand in his sent a jolt of awareness through him.

Ms. Navarre, Dad. She's not married.

As he turned to walk away, Peter hesitated. The woman was beautiful, intelligent and *single*. "Uh, Ms. Navarre…"

Good grief. Suddenly he was thirteen again and asking Cindy Worthington to the Valentine dance. He was a geeky ball of jittery nerves and sweating palms. He hadn't asked a woman on a first date in more than thirteen years. Not since he'd asked Katie out for the first time in high school. Since Katie's death, he'd preferred to be alone, to focus on Patrick and losing himself in his work.

But somehow Lisa Navarre was different from the other women in Honey Creek. She'd managed to stir something deep inside him that had been dormant since Katie died—an interest in getting back into life.

She raised an expectant gaze, waiting for him to continue.

His heart drummed so loudly in his ears, he was sure she could hear it. "I was wondering if you might be free next Saturday to—"

Wham!

A loud thump reverberated through the library, drawing his attention to the front desk. When he saw the source of the noise and the ensuing commotion, he tensed. Maisie Colton was not only a Colton, reason enough for Peter to steer clear of her, but the *Vogue*-beautiful woman was well-known in town as being eccentric and unpredictable.

Maisie angrily slammed another stack of books on the counter, and Lily Masterson rushed over to quiet Maisie.

"No respect!" Maisie steamed, full voice. "Do you know how many times I've called that damn show? And they *still* won't talk to me!"

Lily murmured something quietly to Maisie, who retorted, "The *Dr. Sophie* show, of course. My God, this town has enough dirty secrets and public scandals to fill the show's programming for weeks! But the ninny they have working in PR not only wouldn't listen to me, but told me to stop calling or she'd contact the police!" Maisie tossed her long dark hair over her shoulder and scowled darkly.

Peter gritted his teeth, mentally applauding the *Dr. Sophie* show's PR rep for recognizing a kook when they heard one and having the guts to stand up to Maisie. Not too many people in Honey Creek did. She was, after all, a Colton, and Coltons held a great deal of power in the town.

He knew he should ignore Maisie's outburst as most of the other library patrons were, but watching Maisie Colton was a little like watching a train wreck. Despite knowing better, you just can't look away.

In hushed tones, Lily tried to calm Maisie, but she bristled and railed at Lily, "Don't tell me what to do! This is a public building, and I have every right to be here and speak my mind."

Mary edged up to the front counter to give Lily backup, and Peter groaned. This could get ugly.

Mary spoke quietly to Maisie, and, as he'd predicted, Maisie rounded on his sister in a heartbeat. He heard a hateful, derogatory term thrown at his sister, and he'd had enough. Turning briefly to Lisa Navarre, Peter said, "Excuse me. I have to go." He hustled up to the front desk, where Maisie was bristling like an angry cat, flinging insults at Mary.

"…Walsh slut like your sister! Lucy ruined my brother's life the instant she hooked her talons into Damien and seduced him. I pity poor Jake Pierson. You damn Walshes are all the same!" Maisie huffed indignantly.

Peter stepped up behind his sister, not saying anything but drilling Maisie with a warning look.

"And you!" She aimed a shaking finger at him. "You killed Katie, same as if you'd pulled a trigger."

Peter stiffened, bile churning in his gut. "That's enough, Maisie. Go home."

"She died having your baby! Or don't you care? Your father sure didn't care how many women he hurt, how many hearts he broke, how many lives he ruined!"

Mary gasped softly, and Peter sensed more than saw the shudder that raced through his sister. He stepped forward, prepared to bodily throw Maisie from the library if needed, just as another woman brushed past him to confront Maisie.

Lisa Navarre. Startled, Peter caught his breath, as if watching a fawn step in front of a semi-trailer.

"It's Ms. Colton, right?" Lisa smiled warmly and held her hand out for Maisie to shake. "I don't know if you remember me, but I taught your son Jeremy a couple years ago."

Maisie gaped at Lisa suspiciously, then shook her hand. "Yeah. I remember you. Jeremy loved your class."

"Well, I loved having him in my class. He's such a sweet

boy. Very bright and well-mannered. I know you must be proud of him."

Maisie sent an awkward glance to Lily, Mary and Peter, then tugged her sleeve to straighten her coat. "I am. Jeremy is the world to me."

Lisa smiled brightly. "I can imagine." Then, gesturing with a glance to Mary and Peter, Lisa continued. "Somehow I doubt he'd be happy if he knew you'd been yelling at these nice people, though."

Maisie lifted her chin, her eyes flashing with contempt. "There is nothing nice about these or any of the Walshes." Nailing an arctic glare on Mary, Maisie added, "I'm glad your father is dead. One less Walsh for the world to suffer."

Peter had never struck a woman in his life, but Maisie tempted him to break his code of honor. He squared his shoulders and would have moved in on the hateful woman if Lisa hadn't spread her hand at her side in a subtle signal asking him to wait.

"Ms. Colton, the town is justifiably upset over the murder of Mark Walsh. Emotions are running high for everyone. I know there is a lot of bad blood between your families, but this kind of name-calling and finger-pointing serves no good. Think about Jeremy. I'm sure the last thing he needs is to hear from his friends that you were causing a scene here today."

Maisie crossed her arms over her chest and moisture gathered in her eyes. "Their family has caused me and my brother years of heartache. Damien spent fifteen years in jail for something he didn't do!"

"I'm sorry for that, truly. But do you really think Damien wants you adding salt to the wounds now, or would he rather put the past behind him?" Lisa's calm tone reminded

Peter of the tactful way she'd handled his tirade earlier in the week.

While he hated to consider himself in the same category as Maisie Colton, he had to admire Lisa's people skills. Already Maisie's ire seemed to have cooled. Incredible.

Maisie glanced away and quickly swiped at her eyes before returning a less militant gaze to Lisa. "You're right. I just get so mad when—"

She shook her head, not bothering to finish. Dividing one last cool glare of contempt between Mary and Peter, Maisie tugged the lapels of her overcoat closed and breezed out the front door.

To Peter, it seemed the entire population of the library sighed with relief.

Lisa turned to Peter and twitched a lopsided smile. "I'm sorry. I probably shouldn't have butted in, but—"

"No apology necessary. You handled that…beautifully. You have a real talent for talking people down from the ledge, so to speak."

"If I have a talent, it's simply for keeping a cool head. And, spending most of my day with a room full of rowdy fourth-graders, it is a skill I've practiced and have down to a science."

Peter laughed. "I bet."

"So before…you were saying something about next Saturday?" She tipped her head in inquiry, inviting him to finish what he'd started.

Peter blew out a deep breath. "Right. To say I'm sorry, I'd like to take you to dinner."

Lisa's eyes widened in genuine surprise. "You're asking me out? Like…on a date?"

Somehow the notion of a date seemed to bother her so he backpedaled. "Well, not really a date. I thought you could give me some advice about how to handle all the stuff that's been happening in my family. You know, with Patrick. You aren't the only one who's seen changes in him lately. I'm worried about him, too. I want to help him but… I don't know where to start."

Patrick's teacher eyed him suspiciously. "Hmm. Good cover."

Peter feigned confusion. "Excuse me?"

When she laughed, the sound tripped down his spine and filled him with a fuzzy warmth like the first sip of a good whiskey. "I'd love to go to dinner with you. But—" she held up a finger, emphasizing her point "—it's not a date."

Peter jerked a nod. "Agreed. Not a date."

Yet even as he consented to her terms, a stab of disappointment poked him in the ribs. *Not a date* wasn't what he'd had in mind and seemed wholly insufficient with a woman like Lisa Navarre.

But for now, it would do.

Chapter 4

After setting a time to pick Lisa up on Saturday, Peter ignored Mary's querying looks and got started skimming through the microfiche of old newspapers to see what he could learn about the Coltons. Lisa returned to her table to study, but just knowing she was nearby was enough to distract Peter from his tedious research. He found himself repeatedly glancing in her direction and wondering where they should go for dinner next weekend.

Perhaps a restaurant in Bozeman would be better than the local fare if they wanted to avoid starting rumors. He knew several high-end restaurants in Bozeman that were sure to impress Lisa, but perhaps, for their first date, he should keep things low-key.

Their *first* date? *First* implied there would be more than one, and since Lisa insisted it wouldn't be a *date* at all, he was definitely getting ahead of himself.

Peter drummed his fingers as he scrolled through the want ads and comic strips looking for the local society page.

Who was he kidding? He might be attracted to Patrick's teacher, but he wasn't in the market for a girlfriend. He and Patrick were getting along just fine on their own. Weren't they? Sure, he didn't have as much time to spend with his son as he'd like, but his mom had been more than accommodating, helping him with babysitting most afternoons and evenings when he had to work late.

He hadn't been on a date since Patrick was born, because he didn't want to get involved with anyone. Involvement meant investment. Investment meant attachment, bonds, intimacy. And the deeper the attachment, the deeper the pain when the bonds broke.

Katie had died ten years ago, and he still felt the loss of his first love, his young bride, his son's mother, to his marrow. How could he risk that kind of pain again?

He flicked another glance to Lisa's table in time to see her look up at him. She sent a quick smile before returning to her studies. A funny catch hiccupped in his chest.

He was getting ahead of himself.

Not a date. *Check*.

Shifting his attention back to the microfiche reader, his eye snagged on a headline about a business deal Darius Colton had signed fifteen years ago, buying out another local rancher who was on the verge of bankruptcy. The *Gazette* reporter heralded the move as the kind of bold, risk-taking business move that had grown the Coltons' ranching empire from relative obscurity twenty years earlier.

Peter's jaw tightened. What the newspaper called bold and risk-taking, Peter called greedy and cut-throat. In the 1990s the Coltons had run most of the local ranches out of business, then swooped in to gobble up the smaller ranches and turn their business into a multi-million-dollar enterprise. Forget the fact that Darius Colton turned around and employed the ranchers he bought out, Peter hated the idea of the Coltons having a monopoly in ranching in and around Honey Creek. The size of the Colton ranch gave them too much power in the town, too much influence over the city council. Yet the money they poured into local projects, charities and businesses elevated the Coltons' stature in the eyes of the community. Honey Creek residents loved the Coltons.

At least, all of Honey Creek except the Walshes.

He moved on to the society page featuring Darius and his third wife, Sharon, who had celebrated their anniversary with a huge gala party at their ranch. He scanned pictures of the Colton brood, including Wes, Maisie and Finn mugging for the camera. Next was a candid shot of Brand Colton, Darius's only child with Sharon, eating cake. Nothing helpful there.

Peter scrolled down farther...and froze. The last shot was a picture of Damien and Lucy, arms around each other, gazing into each other's eyes on the dance floor and smiling with pure love and joy.

Peter forgot to breathe. His pulse pounded in his ears as he stared at the photo of his sister with the young man who'd later shredded their family. Damien's relationship with Lucy had been at the root of Mark Walsh's dispute with the Coltons. The teenagers' love affair had been dissected and publicly examined when Damien went to trial for Mark's murder later that year.

Peter swallowed hard, forcing the bile back down his throat. Old news. Rehashing Damien and Lucy's star-crossed relationship didn't help him figure out what happened to his father in 1995. The simple fact that his father's body had been found in Honey Creek this summer meant that Damien had been innocent of the crime for which he'd been convicted.

Or did it? Damien could still be part of the conspiracy that included poisoning Craig. But even if he didn't pull the trigger, Damien could be complicit in the murder of Mark Walsh via a conspiracy with his family for revenge.

Peter paged through several more weeks of newspapers before he found a tidbit about Finn Colton receiving a science award at Honey Creek High School, another society article about Maisie winning a beauty pageant at the state fair rodeo, and a business article about Darius investing in a real-estate deal near Bozeman. Peter blew out a tired breath and kept scanning.

More society-page drivel about Duke Colton dating the prom queen, Darius and Sharon attending the Cancer Society fund-raiser, Finn Colton winning a scholarship… yada yada.

Peter rubbed a kink in his neck, checked his watch. How long had he been at the library? He'd promised his mother he'd only be gone a couple of hours. She'd been eager to get back to the hospital and spend the evening with Craig.

Peter skipped through several more weeks of farm reports, wedding announcements and sales fliers to search the *Gazette*'s reports from the weeks just prior to his father's disappearance and presumed death.

While there was no shortage of information about the Colton sons' achievements and dating exploits, Maisie Colton's leaving town for an extended vacation and Darius Colton's continued ventures in expanding his ranch and real-estate holdings, Peter saw nothing that pointed to a motive for murder.

"Okay, my curiosity finally got the best of me."

Peter jerked his head around at the sound of Lisa's voice.

She wore her coat, held a stack of books and notepads in her arms, and had her purse slung over her shoulder.

He pushed his chair back and shoved to his feet. "You're calling it a day?"

"Yeah. Think so. I have spelling tests to grade before tomorrow." She rolled her eyes. "That and a bowl of tomato soup are my exciting plans for tonight." She nodded toward the film reader. "So what are you up to over here?" She squinted and read the headline he'd stopped on. "Darius Colton Inks Land Deal." Her eyes ticked up to his. "So what else is new? Darius Colton is the king of ranching around here from what I understand. Is that what you're researching?"

Peter frowned. "Lord, no. Trust me, I'm well-versed in how large the Coltons' ranching business has grown. Naw, I was looking for something else."

She hesitated a beat, as if waiting for him to elaborate, before her brow rose with understanding. He wasn't going to say more. "Oh."

"I, uh…can explain more Saturday, but I'd rather not go into it here." He nodded with his head toward the other library patrons.

"I don't mean to pry. You just looked so…*absorbed* by what you were reading. And intensely frustrated at the same time. It's been most intriguing to watch you over the last hour."

She'd been watching him? Interesting.

He grinned. "Sorting through pages of dross looking for the one bit of gold that will turn my case can be very frustrating."

"Ah, Patrick told me you're a private investigator. Is that what you mean when you say *case*? Something you're researching for a client?"

He shoved his hands in the back pockets of his jeans. He

didn't want to lie to her, but the truth was bound to raise more questions than he was prepared to answer. "I am a P.I., yes. Unfortunately, it's not as glamorous as the movies make it seem." He hitched his head toward the microfiche reader. "This…is not business, though. It's personal."

"Oh." Her tone was more embarrassed now, and she shifted the books in her arms from one side to the other. "I'm sorry I interrupted."

He held up a hand. "Don't be. I was just about finished. I need to get home." He paused, then added, "But I'd love to have your thoughts on this project on Saturday. Maybe a fresh perspective is what I'm needing to put the pieces together."

She lifted a shoulder. "I'll do what I can." Backing toward the door, she gave him a warm grin. "Tell Patrick I said hello."

Her smile burrowed into Peter's chest, chasing away the bitterness and chill left by his walk down Colton-memory lane. "I will. See you Saturday."

"That and a bowl of tomato soup are my exciting plans for tonight," Lisa mimicked herself in a goofy voice as she drove home. Rolling her eyes, she groaned and knocked her fist against her forehead. "Could you sound any more pathetic?"

If that line didn't sound like a pitifully obvious hint that she wanted him to ask her out for tonight, then she was Queen Elizabeth. She'd wanted to eat her words the minute she heard the sentence tumble from her lips.

Peter Walsh was probably already regretting their dinner plans on Saturday, wondering what kind of desperate female she was. She'd babbled like a schoolgirl around the football jock.

And maybe she *was* that pathetic. She hadn't dated

anyone since Ray had left her four years ago. The scars from her marriage, her infertility, the angry accusations Ray had flung at her before storming out, still stung. All it took was an innocent question such as "What's behind the career change?" to pick the scabs of the old wounds.

How was she supposed to tell Peter Walsh that being around children all day only rubbed salt in her wounds? As much as she loved teaching, loved her class, loved making a difference in the lives of her young students, being around children all day only reminded her of what she could never have. The one thing she couldn't give Ray. The one thing she could never give any man.

A baby.

Some days she felt as though she wore a scarlet *I* on her forehead, branding her as infertile. A giant warning sign to keep men away.

Then, quite unexpectedly, Peter Walsh had waltzed into her life and planted a seed of hope. He'd seemed genuinely interested in her. And despite their inauspicious first meeting, she liked Peter Walsh, just as Eve had said she would. His gracious apology, his wry humor, his charming grin made her knees weak and her spirits light. He made her forget, for a few foolish moments, why she hadn't dated in four years. She couldn't impose her infertility on another man.

Lisa parked in her driveway and sighed. Her small house, with its gray siding and shutterless windows, seemed especially lonely tonight and the cloudy November sky didn't help her mood.

She'd met a handsome, interesting man this week, the kind of man who should have her hopeful and energized by the possibilities for the future. Yet she refused to give her heart to another relationship only to suffer the same frustrations and the agony of a childless marriage that she'd been through with Ray. Even the friendship she'd had with Ray had been eroded by the tedious tests, the fruitless attempts at in vitro fertilization, one heartbreaking attempt at adoption and the small fortune they'd spent with nothing to show for their efforts. Lisa had decided years ago that a second marriage would surely end as disastrously as the first. Romance and happy endings were for women lucky enough to be fertile.

Thus the no-dating rule. If she didn't date, she couldn't fall in love, couldn't lose her heart to a relationship that could have no future.

Which left her where she was tonight. Eating tomato soup with no other plans but to grade spelling tests. Alone, except for her cranky cat, Samson.

As she entered her house, juggling her stack of textbooks and notes, said cranky feline was asleep on her couch, a big brown ball of Maine coon fluff and attitude.

Lisa set her books on the kitchen counter and walked over to Samson. "Working hard again, I see."

When she ruffled his fur, Samson raised his head and chomped her hand, letting her know he didn't appreciate her sarcasm or having his nap disturbed.

"Ow." Lisa shook her offended hand and chuckled. "Ingrate." Despite his less-than-sunny disposition, she loved her irascible cat, her only company on cold nights like tonight.

Lisa clicked on the televison to fill the house with other voices, then headed back to the kitchen to heat her soup and fix sourpuss his dinner.

Patrick Walsh's spelling test was on the top of the stack of papers she had to grade after dinner. She paused and stared at the boy's neat script.

What were Peter and Patrick doing tonight? Was Peter helping Patrick with his homework or hiding out in a home office or behind a newspaper, cut off from his son? Peter seemed genuinely interested in seeking her advice on how to help Patrick through the family's recent rough patch. Maybe—

She shook her head and pushed the school papers across the counter. She needed to stop dwelling on Peter and Patrick Walsh.

But as the quiet November evening passed, Samson snoozing beside her as she graded tests, Lisa found keeping her mind off Peter and their upcoming dinner was easier said than done.

Peter had difficulty concentrating on his P.I. cases that week. Not only was he anticipating his dinner with Lisa Navarre on Saturday, but he also was plagued by thoughts of his father's unsolved murder and the dead ends he kept running into. On Wednesday afternoon, a comment that Mary had made Sunday at the library filtered through his brain and struck him with an idea. Abandoning the unfaithful-spouse case he'd been working on, he drove over to the new security firm that Mary and Jake Pierson were running to grill his sister.

When he strode into the office, Mary glanced up from the desk where she was working and sent him a bright smile. "Peter, what a nice surprise! Imagine seeing my reclusive brother twice in one week."

"Reclusive?"

She raised a palm. "I just call them as I see 'em. You just don't get out much."

Peter rocked on his heels. "I have a son to take care of and a business to run. Who has time to socialize?"

"Although I did overhear something Sunday about you and Lisa Navarre. What's the story there, big brother?"

"The story is there is no story. And if there was it would be none of your business."

Mary pulled a face and raised her hands in surrender. "Touchy, touchy. Forgive me for being interested in the fact that you've got your first date in ten years."

"It's not a date."

Mary flashed a smug grin. "Sure, it's not."

He scowled and pulled up a chair opposite her. "Can we move on to why I'm here?"

"Why are you here?"

Peter leaned forward, holding his sister's gaze. "On Sunday you mentioned the trouble you encountered when you and Jake looked into Dad's disappearance back in '95. I know about the FBI agent that was killed and that you think Jake was the real target, but did you ever get a sense of who was behind the murder?"

"We know who pulled the trigger. Jake killed him to save me. But he died before he could tell us who hired him, and we've left that case and the arson investigation up to Sheriff Colton."

Peter stiffened. "Arson? Are you telling me the fire at Jake's house wasn't an accident?"

She raised a hand to quiet him. "We're trying to keep that info on the down-low until the person behind all of these attacks on us is caught."

"You should have told me! I'm your brother, for crying out loud!"

She waved a hand of dismissal. "Wes and Perry are looking into the arson angle. There was no point in dragging you into it. And you need to stay out of the investigation now. Give Wes room to work."

"Wes and Perry are *Coltons,* Mary! If a Colton is behind the attacks—"

"Look, I know you don't trust Wes, but Jake does and that's good enough for me."

Another attack involving his family that was unsolved. He was sure this was no coincidence. All the more reason to step up his investigation.

Restless, he scratched his chin and struggled to rein in his thoughts. "Tell me again what Jake found out about Dad and where he went fifteen years ago. Don't leave anything out."

Mary sighed and rubbed her freckled forehead. "There's nothing else to tell you, Peter. Like I said months ago, we found out Dad had a lover in Costa Rica. We know he was there for a while, then…we hit a brick wall."

A shadow crossed Mary's face, and she cut her glance away. Peter knew his sister well enough to know she was hiding something. No surprise. Mary had always had secrets she wouldn't share with him. He'd always figured secrets were part and parcel of having a younger sister. But he hated the idea of her holding back information on something as critical as what had happened with their father fifteen years ago.

He propped an arm on the edge of her desk and canted further forward. "Mary, if our family is in danger, I deserve the whole truth. How can I protect Patrick if I don't know what I'm up against?"

"The best way to protect your son is to leave this investigation alone. There is more at work here than you know, more than I can tell you. You have to believe me when I tell you trustworthy people are working to find our father's killer and straighten out this whole squirrely mess."

"This involves me, too." Peter jabbed the desk with his finger. "I have a right to know what is going on."

Mary gave him a pleading look. "And you will, Peter, as

soon as everyone else knows. But if you investigate on your own, you could ruffle feathers and step on toes that could bring some dangerous people to your front door. Please, Peter, back off. Give up this vendetta you seem bent on. Let the authorities do their job."

"I can't, Mary. Not when the authorities belong to the very family I suspect is behind all of this." Peter shoved to his feet, frustrated by his sister's refusal to help him.

"Wes Colton isn't the enemy. He's doing all he can to solve Dad's murder. Don't you think with all the suspicion hanging over his family ever since Damien was accused of killing Dad years ago that Wes wants to find the *real* culprit and clear his family's name once and for all?"

Peter stormed to the office door and paused with his hand on the knob. "Circumstances may have cleared Damien of murder once, but the Coltons are a large family. They haven't forgiven or forgotten their grudges against our dad any more than you or I have."

Mary's spine straightened, and her face paled. "I may not have forgotten everything Dad did to us and to Mom. But I've moved on. Jake is my future, and I've put the past where it belongs. In the past. For Patrick's sake, I wish you could do the same."

A sharp stabbing sensation arrowed to his chest. Were his complicated feelings toward his father messing up his relationship with Patrick? If anything, Peter had tried hard to be the kind of father Mark Walsh had never been for his children—warm, involved, supportive. He had a good relationship with Patrick, even if his caseload had kept him preoccupied of late. Didn't he?

He stewed over Mary's comment as he drove home. On the heels of Lisa's comment that Patrick needed his father to be more involved in his life, he tried to see his life from Patrick's perspective. They ate breakfast together, but conversation, if any, revolved around Peter hurrying his son and double-checking the usual laundry list of morning requirements—brushed teeth, homework in backpack, lunch money.

In the evening, Patrick spent most of his time in his room playing video games and when he did come out to try to talk to Peter, he got only half of Peter's attention while he read the newspaper or worked on the computer or watched a football game on television. Maybe their time together *didn't* equate to the kind of relationship he thought he had with Patrick.

Peter squeezed the steering wheel. He had to do better. He couldn't repeat the mistakes his father had made. He didn't want Patrick growing up with the kind of distance and disconnect he'd had in his relationship with his father. A distance that grew to resentment.

Although, as Peter got older and realized *why* his father wasn't around, heard rumors of his father's many affairs and shady business deals, resentment became disgust, anger. Hatred.

Yet beneath the bitter layers was the little boy who still craved his father's love and attention. The sharp pang in his chest returned. Patrick would never know that double-edged sword of love and hate if he could help it. Gritting his teeth, Peter resolved to change his habits, rearrange his work schedule, make a conscious effort to give Patrick the attention he needed. Nothing mattered more than his son.

His mother and Patrick were in the yard when he pulled in the front drive. As Peter climbed out of his truck, Patrick loped over and showed him the carcass of a giant beetle he'd found. "Look how big this thing was, Dad!"

His mother, Jolene, gave a shudder. "I'm glad you're home. Big dead bugs are not my cup of tea!"

Peter examined the black beetle and raised an eyebrow. "Impressive, sport. What are you gonna do with it?"

"I should take it to school tomorrow and put it in Missy Haynes's locker!" Patrick laughed. "She'd be so grossed out."

Peter gave his son a firm look. "The bug does *not* go to school. Torturing girls is not gentlemanly behavior."

"Can I take it to show Ms. Navarre for science?"

Just the mention of Lisa's name caused his pulse to kick. "As long as that's all that the bug is used for. No tricks or pranks."

Patrick gave him the universal parents-are-such-a-drag look but nodded. "Okay."

"Better get inside and finish your homework now, Patty-boy," Jolene said, giving her grandson a side-hug. His mother's fiery red hair shimmered with the same orange and gold colors of autumn as the trees in the late-afternoon sun, and her amber eyes shone with her love for her only grandchild.

With a grunt of displeasure, Patrick turned to go inside, dragging his feet through the clutter of dead leaves and slushy snow.

"So," Jolene said, stepping forward to greet Peter with a hug and brief kiss on his cheek, "how was your day?"

"All right, I suppose. Frustrating though. I just can't seem to get anywhere with my investigation of Dad's murder."

Jolene blinked her surprise. "You're doing what? Did the sheriff ask for your help?"

Peter scoffed. "Hell, no. In fact, he warned me away. But Wes Colton sure isn't making any progress finding Dad's killer."

"And you know this how?" Jolene asked, crossing her arms over her chest.

Peter started inside, hitching his head to ask his mother to follow. "Has he given you any reason to think he's learned anything? That he's any closer to an arrest now than he was months ago?"

"Well, no. But then I've been much more concerned with Craig's condition and finding out who poisoned him, who tried to kill Mary."

As they entered the foyer, Peter pitched his voice low to keep Patrick from overhearing. "Craig and I think Dad's killer and the person responsible for the other attacks on the family may be one and the same."

Jolene didn't act surprised. "Craig mentioned his conspiracy theory to me. I didn't realize he'd gotten you involved in investigating it, though."

"He didn't have to ask me. If I'd known the sheriff was going to be so remiss in doing his job, I'd have gotten involved months ago. But maybe Wes's lack of progress is all the evidence we need that a Colton is involved, and Wes is covering for his family."

Jolene pulled off her coat and hung it on the coatrack by the door. "You know I have no love lost for the Coltons myself, but you should be careful throwing around accusations like that. Do you have any proof the Coltons are behind anything that's happened?"

"Nothing I can take to court. But my gut tells me—"

"Peter, your gut is biased. Don't get so focused on taking down the Coltons that you miss evidence right under your nose."

Peter tensed. "What are you saying? Do you know something you haven't told the police?"

She waved him off and moved to the stove to start the kettle heating. "No, nothing like that. Just don't limit your investigation to the Coltons. Plenty of folks had reason to hate your father. He hurt a lot of people." Grief and heartache filled her tone, and Peter heard her unspoken, *including me.*

"Well, if I had other leads I'd follow them, but even Mary is being a brick wall. She won't talk to me about what she found when she and Jake looked into Dad's disappearance back in '95."

His mother faced him with a stern look in her eye. "Don't pester Mary about your father. She's happy, truly happy for the first time in too long."

"I wasn't pestering her. I just wanted to know more about what she and Jake learned. But all she'll say is that Dad went to Costa Rica with a woman before his trail went cold." Peter realized what he'd said and kicked himself mentally. "Sorry. I shouldn't have brought that up."

"What, that your father had other women? Good grief, Peter, I knew about his women well before you kids ever did." Though she tried to dismiss Mark's affairs with a casual brush-off, Peter could see the shadows that crept into her eyes. Knowing about her husband's infidelity didn't mean Jolene Walsh hadn't cared, hadn't been hurt. She turned her back to Peter to pour hot water over the tea bag in her mug.

Peter crossed the kitchen and squeezed his mother's shoulder. "You all right?"

She glanced up, then firmed her mouth and gave a confident nod. "I am. Better than all right, in fact. I've moved on, and I have Craig in my life now."

Peter tugged up a corner of his mouth, wondering what his mother would say if he told her he'd known about her once-secret relationship with Craig for years. In recent months, they'd been more public about their love for each other, and Peter couldn't be happier for her.

Jolene set the kettle back in place and lifted her chin. "Craig's ten times the man your father was, and he makes me feel cherished." She beamed at him. "I'm a blessed woman."

"I agree." Peter kissed his mother's temple then walked to the kitchen table to sort through the day's mail.

"Peter."

He glanced up at his mother and waited for her to blow on her tea before she continued. "This woman down in Costa Rica…"

"Mom, you don't need to—"

She waved a hand to hush him. "Wait a minute. Hear me out." She stared into her mug and knitted her brow. "She was just one in a long line of women your father had. If you ask me, you should look into his liaisons and see who might have motive to kill your father. Maybe one of his women wasn't as willing to overlook his numerous affairs as I was."

Peter rocked on his heels, pondering his mother's suggestion. "But…why would one of Dad's women have any reason to hire Atkins to poison Craig?"

"No one said they did. The two crimes could be unrelated."

"And the attack on Mary and Jake? Did you know the fire at Jake's was arson?"

Jolene shrugged. "I don't know how it all fits. I'm just saying don't get tunnel vision when it comes to the Coltons. Consider everything and everyone."

Peter rubbed a hand over his chin. "Okay, so how do I find the women with whom dad had his 'liaisons,' as you call them. I don't want to cause a ruckus in town by asking women, 'Did you sleep with my father or know anyone who did?'"

Jolene chuckled. "Yeah, that'll go over like a lead balloon."

"And would likely tip off the killer that I'm on his, or

rather her, tracks." He paused. "Unless it was a jealous husband." Pulling a face, Peter shook his head. "Well, you're right about the fact that Dad made plenty of enemies."

From the next room, the sounds of Patrick settling his books on the dining-room table and dragging out a chair to start his homework drifted in.

Jolene set her tea on the counter and stepped closer to Peter. Lowering her voice to barely more than a whisper, she said, "Tess Cantrell."

Peter furrowed his brow, not sure he'd heard correctly. The name didn't mean anything to him. "Who is that?"

"She lives in Bozeman. Your father had a long-term relationship with her just before he disappeared. The only reason I know her name is because she confronted me once many years ago. I think she was hoping that by revealing herself to me, I would be shocked by Mark's affair and divorce him." Jolene paused and arched an auburn eyebrow. "She was the one surprised when I told her not only did I know about Mark's affairs, she was kidding herself if she thought she was his only fling." She gave him a wry grin and an insouciant shrug.

Peter stared at his mother, marveling at her strength and resilience, her ability to make light of a situation that had caused her so much pain in the past. For years she'd endured the humiliation of her husband's perfidy in order to keep her family together and minimize the scandal. She deserved every bit of happiness she'd found with Craig, and then some.

Sticking his hands in his pockets, Peter shot his mother a quizzical look. "And you think this Tess Cantrell could have something to do with Dad's disappearance years ago or his murder a few months ago?"

"I wouldn't know. But she's as good a place to start as

any. Last I knew, she was still living in Bozeman, not far from the apartment Mark kept there for his trysts."

"Dad! Gram!" Patrick hollered from the next room. "Can one of you help me with this stupid math?"

Jolene turned to head into the dining room, but Peter caught her arm. "I've got it. You can go on to the hospital and see Craig. I've taken enough of your day."

"I don't mind. In case you haven't noticed, I'm a little crazy about my grandson."

Peter lifted the corner of his mouth. "I've noticed. And I appreciate the help more than you know. But I've been told recently that I'm not spending enough time with Patrick. Helping him with his homework is a good place to start changing that."

Jolene cocked her head. "Who told you that?"

"Long story." He nudged her toward the door. "Tell Craig I said hello, and I'll keep him posted on any leads."

A knowing gleam sparked in his mother's eyes. "Interesting. You don't want to talk about it. Could it involve a woman? Say, an attractive schoolteacher?"

Peter frowned. "How—" *The library*. "Mary?"

Jolene nodded. "I think it's wonderful that you're finally dating someone."

"We're not dating."

"Not what I heard…" his mother replied in a sing-song tone as she left through the front door, then called, "Bye, Patty-boy!"

Peter dragged a hand down his face. Having a large family in a small town could be a mixed blessing. While he could never have raised Patrick as a single father without his family's ready support, the Walsh grapevine rivaled Eve Kelley's beauty salon for the lightning speed gossip traveled through it.

As he headed into the dining room to help Patrick with

his math, a tangent thought stopped Peter. *Large family in a small town.*

The Coltons.

Were all of the Coltons privy to the rest of the family's secrets? Was there another tack he could use to learn what the Coltons were hiding?

Don't get tunnel vision when it comes to the Coltons. Peter pinched the bridge of his nose. Maybe his mother was right. She had known the Coltons longer than he had and knew more about his father's potential enemies.

Stepping over to a notepad on the kitchen counter he jotted the name *Tess Cantrell* and underlined it.

He stared at the name, and his gut clenched. Did he really want to find and interview his father's former mistress? Now, *that* would be awkward. He was no stranger to questioning witnesses, but Tess Cantrell's relationship with his father made interrogating her deeply personal and potentially painful. And he wasn't the most tactful man alive. He was sure to do something to get the Cantrell woman's back up.

His thoughts flashed to Lisa Navarre's smooth handling of Maisie Colton at the library. Bozeman. Dinner Saturday.

A beat of anticipation and possibility jumped in his veins. Could Lisa Navarre's people skills help him get the information he needed from Tess Cantrell?

Chapter 5

Late Saturday afternoon, Peter arrived at Lisa's house a few minutes earlier than they'd arranged, and she checked her hair in the entry-hall mirror as she hurried to the door. The sight of him, his square-cut jaw and cheeks slightly red from the cold and his broad shoulders filling the door frame, stole her breath. Peter Walsh was a handsome man, no denying. And at that moment, his bedroom eyes, peering at her from under the brim of a black Stetson, and his lopsided grin were directed at her.

"Hope I'm not too early." His breath clouded when he spoke.

"Not a problem." She stood back to usher him inside. "Come in from the cold while I get my purse and coat."

Peter seemed even taller, his shoulders wider, when he stepped into her cramped foyer. A hint of pine-tinged cologne and the leather scent of his suede coat filled the air and hijacked her pulse. The masculine scents that surrounded him reminded her how long it had been since she'd spent time alone with a man.

"I hope it's not inappropriate for me to tell you how nice you look."

Her heart gave a nervous thump. "A lady always appreciates a sincere compliment, Mr. Walsh."

"Peter, please. And I'm completely sincere."

"Thank you." Heat pricked her face as he swept another appreciative gaze over her. "I'll be right back. Make yourself at home." She hoped her voice didn't betray her jitters. Backing down her hall, she turned and scurried to her bedroom to collect her purse. *Deep breath. Settle down. It's not a date.*

"You have a nice house," he called from the front room.

"Thank you. It's small, but it's all I need." Lisa pulled her dress coat from the closet and took her cell phone from her nightstand.

"On the way in, I noticed you had a broken window on the west side and a patch of broken shingles on the roof right above it."

Lisa poked her arms in the sleeves of her coat as she headed back down the hall. "Yeah. Had a branch from my neighbor's tree hit the house during the tornado last month." She reached the living room and caught her breath again at the sight of him. He might be a private investigator but with his Stetson, his suede range coat and his rugged good looks, he could easily be mistaken for one of the ranchers who populated Honey Creek.

She cleared the sudden thickness from her throat. "I've been too busy to call a repairman, and I figured there were folks with bigger repairs than mine first in line following the storm. For now the cardboard fix will have to suffice on the window."

He pointed to the couch where Samson sat staring at Peter. "I don't think your cat likes me. He's been giving me the evil eye since I arrived."

Lisa grinned. "Don't mind him. He acts tough, but under all that fluff, he's just a big marshmallow."

She walked over to scratch the Maine coon under the chin, and Samson gave a loud *mrow* before hopping off the couch and stalking away.

"You know, with this cold weather settling in, you should see about getting the window fixed soon or your heating bill is going to eat your lunch." He crossed to her, lifting a hand for her to proceed him to the door. "If you want, I can take care of those repairs for you. Shouldn't take more than a couple hours one afternoon. Did you have any other damage?"

Lisa led him out to her front stoop and paused long enough to lock her door. "No, the branch was about the extent of it, thank goodness. Other folks weren't as lucky." She flashed him a smile as they walked to his truck. "And though I appreciate the offer, I couldn't ask you to do my repairs."

"You didn't ask. I offered." He opened the passenger door for her and sent her a sheepish look. "Besides, I have a favor to ask you, and doing a few repairs for you is the least I can do to repay you."

Lisa lingered in the open door, enjoying standing so close to Peter's body heat and his tempting masculine scent, and she tilted her head. "What kind of favor?"

"I, uh…have a side trip I need to make tonight before dinner. Business-related." He paused and firmed his mouth. "Actually, it's more personal business." He knocked his Stetson back and scratched his forehead, stalling.

She gave him a patient smile of encouragement. "What's the favor, Peter?"

"I have to interview a woman in Bozeman. She had a, uh…a relationship with my father when I was a kid, and…I think she might have information that would help me find the person responsible for my dad's murder."

Lisa frowned. "Why aren't the police talking to her then?"

"She's not a suspect or anything. I'm just following a hunch, tracking down any possible leads. I'm conducting my own investigation into recent events. This has nothing to do with the case the sheriff's building." He hitched a shoulder. "Unless I find something significant."

Lisa drew a deep breath of the crisp autumn air. "And you want me to help you somehow?"

"I saw how you handled Maisie Colton at the library the other day. You're good with people and—"

Lisa chuckled her surprise, then covered her mouth with her hand. "I'm sorry. I don't mean to laugh. I've just never considered myself a "people" person. If you knew how nervous I get about talking to parents, how nervous I am even right now—" She stopped and swallowed hard.

Oops. Maybe she shouldn't have said *that*.

Sure enough, when she ticked her gaze up to Peter's, his eyes were warm, and a grin tugged his cheeks. "Don't be nervous. Remember, this isn't a real date."

The low, husky quality of his voice made her quiver low in her belly. Goose bumps that had nothing to do with the nip in the air rose on her arms.

She twitched a grin. "Right. Not a date."

"So will you help guide the conversation and smooth the rough edges for me when I talk to Tess Cantrell? Knowing that she was my father's former lover makes me more than a little uncomfortable."

"I can imagine." Lisa raised her chin and squared her shoulders. "I'd be happy to help however I can."

The smile of gratitude and relief that spread across Peter's face was all the reward she needed, but Peter still insisted he would tend to her home repairs later that week.

As they drove to Bozeman, Peter filled her in on the recent turbulence in the Walsh family. Besides the death of Mark Walsh, a tragedy she was familiar with only through the reports in the *Honey Creek Gazette,* Peter's sister had been forced off the road, her fiancé's house torched. Then a close family friend, a man Peter considered a second father, had been hospitalized after being poisoned.

"And you think all the incidents are related?" Lisa gave him a skeptical frown. Honey Creek had its share of petty crime, but the kind of conspiracy to commit multiple murders seemed a bit much for their small town.

"I can't prove it yet, but I intend to. Thanks to my line of work, I've learned not to believe in coincidence. Generally, if someone in your life is acting suspiciously, there's usually a reason." Peter glanced across the front seat to her. "Three attacks on my family in four months is no coincidence."

An uneasy flutter stirred in her belly. "Do you think you and Patrick are in danger?"

A muscle in his jaw bunched as he gritted his teeth. "I can't say for sure, but I wouldn't rule it out. I can take care of myself, but I'd appreciate it if you kept a close eye on Patrick when he was at school."

"Of course." She nibbled her bottom lip as she studied Peter's profile. "So how have you explained all the recent trouble for the family to Patrick?"

Drawing his eyebrows together low over his eyes, Peter shot her a dubious look. "I haven't told him anything. He's a kid. I didn't want him worried or upset."

Lisa gaped at Peter. "Nothing? You've told him nothing?"

"Well, when his grandfather was found murdered, I had

to tell him about that. It was in the newspaper and all the talk around town. I didn't want him to hear about it from someone else. But he didn't go to the funeral. I figured it would be the media circus it proved to be."

"So he doesn't know about Mr. Warner being in the hospital or the attack on your sister?" Lisa gripped the armrest, goggling over what Peter had shared. No wonder Patrick was acting so withdrawn, so insecure.

Peter rolled up his palm on the steering wheel. "Well… he knows Craig is in the hospital, because my mom babysits Patrick, and she leaves our house to go sit with Craig in his hospital room. But nothing about the arsenic. I told Patrick Craig was just feeling a little ill and was in for tests. Which is the truth…in a sense."

Lisa sighed and laced her fingers in her lap. "Peter, may I be candid?"

He sent her a startled look. "Please."

"I think keeping Patrick in the dark is causing more harm than good. He's a bright boy, and he's old enough to sense when there's unusual stress and upheaval in the family. I think the reason he's been withdrawn lately at school, the reason he made the comment he did about you not caring about him and the reason he decided to act out the other day is that he's feeling excluded, shut out."

Dark clouds filled Peter's expression. "I didn't tell him, because I was trying to protect him."

"I understand that. I'm not telling you this to point an accusing finger. But the other day at the library you asked for my help with your son. I feel like it's my duty as his teacher to look out for his best interests."

He whipped his head toward her. "No, it's my job as his *father* to look out for his best interests. That's what I thought I was doing!"

"We *both* want what's best for Patrick. But that doesn't mean we have to be at cross purposes."

Peter heaved a sigh, sent her a concerned glance and nodded. "You're right. So…go on. I'm listening."

Lisa stretched the fingers of one hand with the other, fidgeting as she gathered her thoughts. "Well, my guess would be he's worried because he knows you're worried, but he doesn't understand why. The underlying tension in the house, the extra time you have to spend away from home, and the hints he picks up about trouble facing the family are all affecting his performance at school. And his mental well-being. He senses something is wrong, and without any explanation from you, he fills in the blanks for himself. He's scared, uncertain. Knowing fourth-graders the way I do, I suspect he's probably thinking the problems are his fault."

"His fault? No…" Peter shot another deeply worried glance at her before returning his attention to the road.

"I know they're not, but he doesn't. Just think how his young imagination must be running wild, conjuring up all form of frightening possibilities to explain the grim mood in your house."

He shook his head and frowned. "If something is bothering Patrick, he knows he can come to me with it. We've always had that kind of open communication between us."

"You mean until recently?" Lisa met Peter's startled look. "You just said you weren't telling him about the family's recent crises. Communication is a two-way street. How can you expect him to be honest and forthcoming with you if you aren't with him?"

"That's different. There are things kids don't need to know. Things he's too young to hear, too young to grasp."

"True. So give them to him on a level he can understand. Weed out the stuff he's too young to hear. But don't pretend nothing is happening and that everything is fine when it's not. You don't have to be gloom and doom. That *will* scare him. But be honest with him and let him know that he's not to blame and that you are still there for him, protecting him. Give him back his sense of security. Let him know you love him and that you'll handle the trouble facing the family together."

Peter said nothing for a while, clearly mulling over all she'd laid out for him. As they neared the Bozeman city limits, he turned to her with a gentle smile. "That makes a lot of sense. Thank you, Ms. Navarre."

"Lisa."

His eyes warmed, and a flutter stirred deep inside her.

"Lisa." He quirked a wry grin. "So if you don't have kids of your own, how'd you get so smart about parenting?"

He meant the question to be teasing and light-hearted. She could see that much in the playful spark in his eyes, the devilish grin tugging his lips.

But his words sent a sharp ache straight to her heart.

So if you don't have kids of your own...

She swallowed the knot that rose in her throat and forced a smile to her face. She would not, would *not* let him see how his innocent words had slashed through her. Curling her fingers into fists, she sucked in a calming breath to steady her voice. "Six years of teaching and a minor in college in child psychology. I thought it would be a good complement to my teaching certificate."

"That'd do it," he replied with a wink.

Fighting down the grief that threatened to spoil her mood, she focused her attention on the Rocky Mountains silhouetted against the setting sun, beyond the lights of Bozeman. Montana had a rugged beauty and majesty that never failed to take her breath away. When Ray had left her, she'd never once thought of leaving Montana and going back to Texas, where her family lived. Even when the ice and snows of winter buried Honey Creek, Lisa saw the landscape as a wonderland.

"When we get to Tess Cantrell's apartment, just follow my lead, okay? I need her to feel comfortable enough to speak freely with me, to tell me everything she remembers about my dad and any enemies he had when she knew him."

Lisa angled her body back to face Peter. In the fading daylight, his profile had the same rugged appeal as the Rockies.

Peter rubbed a hand over his jaw. Although she could tell he'd shaved before he picked her up tonight, the calluses on his palms still scraped against the rugged cut of his chin with a soft scratching sound. Lisa's nerve endings crackled, imagining those wide, rough palms gliding over her skin.

Her mouth dried, and she gave herself a mental shake. Peter Walsh might be handsome as the devil, but entertaining any notions of a physical relationship was…dangerous. She didn't believe in casual sex, and a deeper, more personal relationship could only end badly. Ray was proof enough of what men thought of sterile women. Though most men would deny it until they were blue in the face, the ancient biological imperative to procreate still ruled men on some subconscious level. That primitive drive would eventually rear its head with any man she got involved with and cause the kind of resentment that had ruined her marriage to Ray.

Leaning her head back on the seat, she gave Peter another surreptitious scrutiny. He might be off limits in reality, but my-oh-my, Peter Walsh was fodder for some pretty steamy daydreams.

"This is it," he said, pulling his truck into the parking lot of a sprawling apartment complex and yanking her out of her musings.

While she gathered her purse from the floorboards, Peter circled the truck to open her door for her. He offered her a hand to help her down from the high front seat, and Lisa's heart tap-danced as his large hand closed around hers. Secure. Warm. Strong.

"Is Ms. Cantrell expecting us?"

"No. I didn't want her to have a chance to get cold feet and bolt on us before we arrived."

"You really think this meeting will go that poorly?" Lisa fell in step beside him, and Peter placed a hand on her back, guiding her around a pothole in the sidewalk.

"My father was a brilliant businessman. He built the family brewery into a thriving business. But I'm afraid that's the kindest thing I can say about him. He left a trail of broken hearts and ill will. I'm not expecting much different with Ms. Cantrell."

Lisa read the tension that crept into Peter's face, creasing his forehead and tightening lines around his mouth. She wondered briefly if Peter, like his father, had left a trail of broken hearts. Eve Kelley told her he'd married his high-school sweetheart. But how much had he dated since his wife's death?

They mounted the steps to the second floor and found apartment 208. Peter hesitated, staring at the door with a troubled expression for long seconds.

Lisa's heart went out to him, and she wrapped her hand around his and squeezed. When he glanced at her, startled by her gesture, she smiled her encouragement.

Peter returned a dubious grin. "Guess this won't get any easier by stalling, huh?"

Squaring his shoulders, he knocked firmly and raised his chin to wait. The door was answered promptly by an attractive dark-haired woman whose age Lisa estimated at around fifty-five.

She gave them a friendly, if curious, look. "Yes?" Then Tess Cantrell's gaze froze on Peter, and her smile faded, replaced by wide-eyed dismay. She raised a hand to her mouth and took a step backward. "Oh, my God."

"Tess Cantrell?" Peter asked. "My name is Peter W—"

"Walsh," Tess finished for him. "I see your father in you. The resemblance is…uncanny."

Hearing that he looked like his father didn't seem to sit well with Peter. He stared at Tess Cantrell with a furrowed brow and a stunned expression.

Lisa stepped forward and extended her hand. "I'm Peter's friend, Lisa Navarre. Would you mind if we spoke to you inside for just a moment? We promise not to take much of your time."

Both Tess and Peter rallied when Lisa spoke. Tess shook her hand and gave her a tight smile, then stepped back to invite them in.

"I heard about your father's murder. I wish I could say I was sorry to hear of his death, but… I can't. I was more shocked, really. I thought he'd died fifteen years ago."

Peter grimaced. "We all did."

"I didn't do it, if that's what you're here to ask." Tess closed the door and faced them with her hands on her hips. "Though I'd like to congratulate the person who *did* kill him."

Peter sucked in a breath, his nostrils flaring.

Feeling the tension rising in the room, Lisa jumped in,

hoping Peter would forgive her if she was overstepping her boundaries.

"Ms. Cantrell, we know Mark Walsh hurt a lot of people, and we're not here to make excuses for him or point fingers of blame. But we need information that we think you might have. Because you were involved with Mark Walsh just before his disappearance in 1995, you have a unique perspective on his state of mind, his activities and the people he had business with."

Tess moved past them and took a seat in her living room without inviting them to join her. She stared at the floor with a dark, distant expression, as if recalling past hurts. "What do you want to know?"

"I need a glimpse of my father's life before he disappeared." Peter stepped into the living room and sat on the edge of the couch. "Do you remember him mentioning anyone he was having trouble with? Anyone who was angry with him for some reason?"

She gave them a bitter laugh. "Where do I start? He didn't talk much about his business dealings with me, but more than once we had our dinner interrupted in restaurants by someone who had a bone to pick with your father."

"What do you think happened in '95? Could someone have tried to kill him and botched it? Is that what sent him into hiding? Did he ever mention leaving, ditching his life and making a fresh start?" Peter fired his questions in rapid succession, not giving Tess a chance to answer.

Lisa sidled onto the sofa beside Peter and laid a hand on his knee. He cast a puzzled look to her hand then raised his gaze to meet hers, and with her eyes, she silently warned him to slow down and not push Tess.

"Like I said, I didn't know much about his business life. He always spent a lot of time on the phone talking to his office or working on some new deal, but he was real private about what he was doing. I gave him space to conduct his business and never asked questions. That's not what our relationship was about."

The unspoken what-their-relationship-was-about hung in the air like a specter for the span of a tense heartbeat. Peter grunted churlishly under his breath, and Lisa squeezed his knee to hush him.

Tess apparently heard him, too. She sat straighter in her recliner and lifted her chin. "I make no apologies for the way I lived my life back then. Maybe I was naive to believe all the things Mark Walsh told me, but I did. I gave him the benefit of the doubt more times than I can count. But I honestly thought he cared about me. I loved him, and to me, that was all that mattered."

"Why?"

Peter's question surprised Lisa, and based on her confused and offended expression, it caught Tess off guard as well.

"Excuse me?"

Peter's dark eyes were shadowed, sad. Not hostile. "Why did you love him? What did you see in him?"

Lisa's chest contracted. Peter's expression reminded her of a young boy looking for some reason to cling to hope, some shred of evidence that his father hadn't been the disappointment he remembered.

Tess blinked rapidly and toyed with the charm on her necklace. "He treated me well, made me feel special. He told me things I wanted to hear, bought me presents. We laughed together and traveled together and had great sex."

Lisa felt the sudden tensing of Peter's muscles under her hand.

"He told me he loved me, and I ate it up. Looking back, I can see how shallow I was being. How easily I bought into his lies. We were together for three years before I learned the truth."

"What truth?" Lisa asked.

"He was never gonna leave his wife. He was using me. Didn't really love me the way he said. Maybe he cared in his own way, but I wasn't the love of his life, the way he was mine." She huffed indignantly. "I wasn't even his only woman." She waved a hand toward Peter. "And I don't mean your mother. I knew Mark was married. I mean the young tootsie he was seeing behind my back. Lord only knows how many others there were. But when I found out about the other woman being pregnant with his baby—"

Peter jerked.

"—I gave Mark an ultimatum. Me or her. He said he couldn't dump—"

"Whoa, whoa, *whoa!*" Peter shot to his feet, his body tense. "Back up."

Lisa's pulse kicked up. Not only did mention of pregnancies and babies always set her on edge, but she could tell by Peter's expression, Tess had just dropped a bomb on him.

"What other woman?" he asked hoarsely. "What *baby?*"

Chapter 6

Tess gave him a wary look. "You didn't know?"

Peter's jaw tightened, his eyes widening with shock.

Before he could respond, Lisa rose and wrapped her hand around his wrist. Shoving down her own raw emotions regarding pregnancies, she flashed Tess a smile. "I'm sorry. You've caught us by surprise. Obviously Peter didn't know, and this is a rather big bombshell for him to absorb. I… what can you tell us about this other woman and her baby?"

Tess shifted on the recliner, clearly uncomfortable with the direction of the conversation and eyeing Peter cautiously. "Just that whoever she was, their relationship was a big secret. And I'm not talking secretive like we were. I mean, big-time scandal and hush-hush. And he warned me not to try to find her or confront her because she was…what was the word he used? Oh, yeah…*volatile*. He said she tended to get really possessive and emotional and could be overly dramatic. He was having to dance really fast to deal with her once she found out she was pregnant. He didn't want anything to do with her baby and was already regretting having messed with this woman. He called her 'one of his worst mistakes.'"

"So you don't know her name?" Peter asked, his tone remarkably calm.

Tess shook her head, then sighed heavily. "So when I gave him the ultimatum, he said, 'No one is going to tie me down. Not you and not her.' And he left. Just like that. Never heard from him again." She firmed her mouth and squared her shoulders, but her eyes reflected her warring bitterness and pain.

Lisa moved closer to Tess and crouched next to her chair. She put a sympathetic hand on the other woman's. "I'm sorry. I know this is difficult for you, and we appreciate your candor."

Tess sniffed loudly and nodded.

"Do you think this woman, whoever she is, could have been upset enough to seek retaliation against Mark?" Lisa asked.

Tess lifted a shoulder. "If she was as much of a loose cannon as Mark said, who knows? But I know she was as determined to keep her child's paternity a secret as Mark was. He told me that much. Did she try to kill him to keep her secret?" Tess turned her palm up. "Did she run him out of town to keep him quiet?" Another shrug.

Peter paced across the room, his face grave, then he turned toward Tess, inclining his head in inquiry. "Do you think he could have gone to Costa Rica with her? Set her up there with a house?"

"Costa Rica?" She frowned. "No. As far as I know she stayed in Honey Creek and had the baby."

Peter jolted again, his mouth agape. "Honey Creek? She's from *Honey Creek?*"

Lisa could practically see the wheels in Peter's mind spinning, trying to figure out which woman from his hometown had given birth to his half-sibling.

Tess pushed to her feet now and moved restlessly across the floor. "After Mark left me, I didn't care what happened to the highfalutin' floozy he got pregnant. The crazy woman and her baby were not my problem."

Peter was staring out the front window, his expression shell-shocked, so Lisa continued to carry the questioning. She fumbled to decide what else might be relevant to Peter's investigation, what information Tess might have about Mark's enemies that she didn't realize she had.

"Ms. Cantrell, I know you said Mark didn't discuss his business deals with you, but can you remember a time during the years you were together when he seemed especially worried or upset over a deal? Did he ever indicate a deal had gone wrong and he had to handle the repercussions?"

Tess's shoulders sagged, and she rubbed her neck tiredly. "No. He was always upbeat about his brewery. It was thriving and growing and making him a ton of money. He even started branching out into new industries. He'd started dabbling in oil and ranching, anything he thought he could make a profit on."

Ranching. If Mark Walsh was moving in on Darius Colton's domain, there could have been trouble there. Lisa glanced toward Peter to gauge whether he'd drawn the same conclusion, but his expression was inscrutable.

Finally Tess stopped her restless shuffling and faced them with a determined set in her jaw. "Look, I don't know what else I can tell you. I had nothing to do with Mark's disappearance or his murder. I haven't seen or talked to him in fifteen years." She turned fully toward Peter. "But I can tell you this. You kids were important to him. He wouldn't divorce your mother because he wanted to keep your family together. He didn't want to lose the right to see his children. He loved you…in his own way."

Peter's face reflected a mix of skepticism and longing. The poignant battle of his emotions tugged Lisa's heart.

A gasp from Tess brought Lisa's attention back to the older woman. Tess snapped her fingers and waved a finger. "I just thought of something. In the months before he left, he was real upset about Lucy."

"Lucy?" Lisa asked.

"My sister," Peter supplied. His face said Tess's revelation was old news.

"Lucy was dating some boy he thought was trouble. He said he laid down the law to her that she couldn't see him, but he knew she was sneaking around behind his back."

Peter sighed and shoved his hands in his coat pockets. "Damien Colton."

Recognition lit Tess's face. "I know that name."

"He's who they charged with Dad's murder fifteen years ago." Peter shuffled toward the door, signaling an end to the conversation. "But since my dad wasn't actually dead, but in hiding, Damien just got a get-out-of-jail card from the state. So, thanks, but…that doesn't help."

Tess spread her hands. "I've got nothing else."

Lisa nodded and moved close enough to grasp the woman's hands. "Thank you. For your time and for indulging us when we stirred up bad memories. You have been a big help, and we appreciate what you've told us."

Perhaps because he felt taken to task by her example, Peter also mustered a smile for Tess Cantrell. "Yes, thank you." He dug in his pocket and extracted a business card.

"If you do think of anything else you feel could be helpful, will you call me? Please."

Tess stared at the card for a moment then nodded. "Sure. And I hope for your sake that they catch whoever did it."

With that, Peter opened the front door and stood back while Lisa pulled her coat tighter around her and stepped outside.

The cold slap of the evening air matched Peter's mood as they drove to the restaurant from Tess's apartment.

"If you'd like to skip dinner tonight, I'd understand. You've just been handed a shock, and I can imagine—"

"I'm fine." He added a tense smile that contradicted his assurances. "And I'd still like your input about Patrick."

"My analysis of the problem on the drive to Ms. Cantrell's didn't scare you off, then?" Lisa kept her tone light, hoping to establish a less serious tone for the rest of the evening.

"Not a bit. You were dead on target, and I need all the candor and honesty I can get. Patrick means everything to me, and I'll do whatever it takes to protect him and give him a good childhood."

"I'm guessing your relationship with your dad wasn't so hot when you were a kid?"

"You'd be right. Although at the time, I really didn't know any better. I just knew something was missing in our relationship that other guys had with their fathers. I want to be sure Patrick doesn't grow up feeling the same way."

Peter pulled in and parked at a locally owned restaurant whose sign out front claimed they served the best steaks in the state.

"Best in the state?" Lisa lifted her eyebrows. "Pretty bold claim considering the size of Montana. And this *is* ranching country."

Peter sent her a devilish lopsided grin. "Prepare to be impressed."

He escorted her inside and gave his name to the hostess. Once they'd been seated at a private corner booth, Peter ordered them a bottle of merlot and settled back in his seat. His gaze drifted around the classic Western-themed decor of the restaurant, but Lisa could tell by his deliberative expression that his thoughts were elsewhere.

"So, what do you recommend?" She unfolded her menu and began studying the entree choices.

Peter's dark eyes shifted to her. "I always get the ribeye." He quirked a grin. "Best in the state."

Lisa chuckled. "So I hear."

His face sobering, he leaned toward her and lowered his voice. "Do you think the woman my dad got pregnant actually had the baby?"

Lisa set the menu aside and considered his question. "Why wouldn't she?"

Peter flipped up his palm. "Well, you heard Tess. His affair with this lady was super-secret, and my dad called the woman *volatile*. If she *was* trying to keep his paternity and their relationship a secret, what better way than to get rid of the baby?"

The thought of someone ending a pregnancy when she and Ray had so desperately wanted a baby and couldn't have one made Lisa's chest contract. She fumbled with her napkin, then, seeing her hands shaking, she laced her fingers tightly in her lap. "I suppose it's possible. It's just difficult for me to imagine anyone *not* wanting a baby, even if the circumstances are less than ideal."

Peter nodded, his expression thoughtful. "Assuming she did have the baby, the kid would be…what, fourteen now?" He dragged a hand down his cheek and blew out a deep breath. "I could have a half-sibling out there somewhere."

"Tess said the woman was from Honey Creek. Can you think of anyone who fits the description she gave? Emotional. Desperate to keep their relationship secret."

"With a kid who is now fourteen…yeah. A couple of possibilities come to mind. Lily Masterson for one."

Lisa blinked her surprise. "The new librarian? I thought she just moved to town."

"Moved back to town. She lived here years ago. Had a reputation that even high school boys like me knew about. She was a wild one back then." He hesitated, drawing his eyebrows together in a frown. "She's involved with Wes Colton now. If she had my dad's baby, if she was involved with my dad's disappearance or his death in some way…" Peter gritted his teeth, his dark eyes flashing. "I bet Wes knows about it. He could be covering for her. Seems mighty convenient that Lily shows up back in town at the same time my dad winds up dead."

"Whoa! Slow down." Lisa held her hands up. "Let's not convict her without a little more evidence. You said there was more than one possibility. Who else could it be?"

Peter picked up his spoon and tapped it idly on the table. Suddenly he tensed, and his complexion paled. "Ah, hell."

"What?"

"Maisie Colton. Her son is the right age, isn't he?"

Lisa did a quick calculation. "Yes, but just because her child is the right age—"

"She's also as good as Honey Creek royalty, being a Colton. Our families have been at odds for years. A relationship with my father would be beyond scandalous. And she's—" Peter laughed without humor. "Well, you saw how she acted at the library the other day. She's definitely volatile. Some people say she's borderline nuts."

"And she's gorgeous. I could understand your father falling for her."

Peter gave her a startled look. "Yeah, I suppose she's attractive. I never really thought about it before."

She cocked her head skeptically. "You never noticed that Maisie Colton is drop-dead beautiful? I don't buy it."

Peter leaned closer as if about to confide a dark secret. "She's a Colton." His tone said his statement was self-explanatory.

She waved him off. "Whatever. So there are at least two possibilities. And nothing says the woman, whoever she is, is even still in Honey Creek."

Peter flopped back against the booth again. "You have a point. But it's worth looking into. But could the complication of an unwanted pregnancy be motive for murder?"

Lisa's stomach flip-flopped. "I don't know. Children are a highly charged subject. A lot of very important decisions get made based on having a child with someone." She dropped her eyes to her plate and added under her breath, "Or not."

The waiter arrived with their wine and a basket of rolls, distracting Peter from the comment that had slipped out almost on its own. She hoped he hadn't heard her aside, but Peter's curious gaze stayed fixed on her, as if he were trying to decipher a puzzle, as he ordered their dinners. When the waiter left the table, the question she'd read in Peter's expression came.

"What does *or not* mean?"

Lisa sighed. "I shouldn't have said anything. I was… letting personal history sideline me. Forget it."

But his dark eyes narrowed on her, sharp and intuitive.

"Do you…have a child who's affected decisions you've made?"

Lisa's mouth dried, and she had to clear her throat in order to make her voice work. "In my case, it was the children we *didn't* have that had an impact. The children…I couldn't have. My husband and I divorced after five years of trying to have a baby."

His penetrating gazed softened, and he sat back, looking a bit poleaxed. "Oh." His mouth opened and closed, his struggle to find the right words obvious. "I'm sorry."

Lisa awkwardly forced a laugh. "Wow, talk about a conversation killer." Avoiding his sympathetic but uneasy expression, she fidgeted with the stem of her wine glass, her hand shaking. "Note to self—infertility and subsequent divorce are not fodder for first-date table talk."

Peter's hand closed around her fumbling fingers, and the warmth of his grasp tripped her pulse. With her breath stuck in her lungs, she darted her gaze back to his.

"I thought you said this wasn't a date." The hint of a grin twitched at the corner of his mouth, and his voice was a low, smooth rumble like approaching thunder.

A tingle raced over her skin. The piercing intensity returned to his eyes, shooting heat straight to her core. "I—It's not. I meant…"

His thumb stroked her wrist where her pulse fluttered. "Would a date with me really be such a bad thing?"

A nervous laugh hiccupped from her throat. "No. I just—" Unable to think clearly with the crackle of energy from his touch short-circuiting her brain, Lisa reluctantly pulled her hand from his. Drawing a breath, she gathered her composure. "I don't date. It has nothing to do with you. I just don't think I should get involved with *any* man."

He scrunched his face in disbelief. "Why on earth not? You're young and beautiful and—"

"Peter." She held up a hand to cut him off. "Thank you. I'm flattered, but…none of that changes the fact that…I can't have children." Her shoulders drooped. She really didn't want to get into this discussion. Why had she cracked the door on the topic with her stupid muttering?

He leaned toward her again. "I don't mean to be insensitive, but…I don't see why that should make any difference."

His tone was so gentle it brought tears to her eyes. Or maybe it was the reminder that nights like tonight, alone with a handsome, attentive man, could never be anything more that made her well up. She swallowed the knot of emotion that rose in her throat and blinked away the moisture blurring her vision.

"The only thing more difficult than having Ray walk out on our marriage was seeing the disappointment in his eyes every time an in vitro attempt failed. Not having the children I wanted hurt badly enough, without knowing how I'd let the man I loved down, too. I refuse to put another man through that pain. And… I can't put myself through the heartache of another childless relationship. So…" She paused and squared her shoulders again, reinforcing her words. "I've made it my policy not to start anything I know can't go anywhere."

Lisa held Peter's gaze, her heart thundering as if waiting for an official judgment to be passed down.

A muscle ticked in his jaw as, for several nerve-racking moments, he silently studied her with a shadowed expression. Finally, in a husky voice that slid over her like a lover's caress, he said, "I'm sorry to hear that. Because I think you're special, and…I'm very attracted to you. I'd have liked the chance to…get to know you better."

His deep timbre and the hungry look in his eyes said

he wanted to do much more than "get to know" her. The answering shimmy low in her belly concurred.

If she'd thought she could have meaningless sex simply to satisfy the feverish ache Peter stirred deep inside her, maybe she'd take him up on the promise implicit in his dark, seductive eyes.

Lisa squeezed the armrests of her chair, holding herself in place as the maelstrom of tangled emotions blasted through her. On the heels of her frank confession about her infertility and the shared shock of learning Peter had a half-sibling, the temptation to lose herself in mind-numbing sex pounded through her like a gale-force wind.

But sex could never be meaningless for her, and hiding from the harsh realities of her circumstances was not her style, even if spending a night in Peter's arms did hold great appeal. Her raw honesty had already created a sense of intimacy between them that was dangerous to her heart. Under other circumstances, Peter Walsh was just the kind of man she'd like to 'get to know,' too.

The waiter arrived with their food, allowing Lisa to shake herself from the hypnotic lure of Peter's gaze. But not even the 'best steak in the state' could satisfy the cravings Peter had revived in her tonight—the desire to be held in strong arms, the yen to share her life with someone, and the bittersweet longing for a child of her own.

Peter sipped his wine and studied Lisa over the rim of his glass. He shouldn't have pushed her to divulge the painful reasons behind her divorce, but after only a few hours in her company, he felt himself powerfully drawn to her and wanted to get past her no-dating rule. Considering his own reluctance to involve himself with a woman since Katie's death, his attraction to Patrick's teacher had blindsided him.

Was he ready to take the risks that came with dating? He had more than his own interests to think about now. What was best for Patrick? He and Patrick had been alone for so long, what would it do to their relationship to add a woman to the mix? And was the lack of a mother figure in Patrick's life at the root of his son's recent problems?

Peter cleared his throat before diving into the subject of his son. "So you promised to help me figure out what to do about Patrick. Your suggestion that I explain more of what's happening with the family is a start, but…the truth is, I've felt a distance growing between us for more than a year now. We used to be really close. We did everything together but now…he's pulling away."

Lisa held his gaze, listening attentively as she cut a bite of steak.

"Nowadays, he'd rather sit in his room and play video games than talk to me."

She smiled. "I think most kids his age are more interested in playing video games or sports than talking to their parents. He's ten, Peter. He's a preteen, and it's natural for him to start establishing some independence at his age."

"Preteen?" Peter let his wrist fall heavily to the table and groaned. "God, I hadn't thought about that. What am I going to do with a teenager?"

Lisa chuckled. "Scary as it sounds, you will survive."

"I just wonder sometimes if I've done enough, if I've been a good enough parent. I can't always be there and when Patrick starts doing things that are out of character for him—" he nodded toward Lisa "—like acting out at school, I feel like I've failed."

Lisa shook her head. "You haven't failed. Patrick is a great kid. He's bright and well-behaved…usually. He's a pleasure to have in my class. But his recent mood changes tell me he's just going through a difficult adjustment. Maybe because of the trouble your family has encountered, maybe because you've been working longer hours lately…"

Peter's gaze snapped up to hers. "He told you that?"

"No, you did. The day you came up to the school."

He scratched his chin slowly. "To be honest, I don't remember much of what I said. Only that I was pretty short with you." He sent her an apologetic look. "I'd just been at the hospital to visit Craig Warner, and we'd been discussing the recent chain of trouble my family's been going through. Discussing the fact that we believe the events are connected." Peter elaborated briefly on the attack on Mary, Craig's relationship with the family and his poisoning and the discovery of Mark Walsh's body. Lisa's expression reflected her growing concern and dismay for all the Walshes had endured.

"When I came to the school, I took my frustrations with the case out on you. I'm sorry."

"You've already apologized. The issue we need to solve is how do you reach out to Patrick during all of this, so he's not hurt by the ripple effects of these family problems."

Peter spread his hands. "I'm all ears. What do you suggest?"

"Well, the football game you took him to last weekend was a good start. He beamed like a Christmas light when he told me about the game on Monday."

Peter smiled. "I'm glad he had fun."

She leaned forward, her expression direct and serious. "I'd dare to say it wasn't the game nearly as much as the time with you that he enjoyed. You need to make an effort to do things with him outside of your normal routine. I know that's hard when you are a single parent with a busy job. But for Patrick's sake, try to *make* time."

Peter filled his lungs and nodded. "I can do that. Any ideas?"

"Well…" Lisa stabbed a bite of potato and flashed him a cagey glance. "I have an idea that is self-serving."

Intrigued, Peter arched an eyebrow. "Do tell."

"I'm in charge of the Fall Festival at school. We were supposed to have it last month, but the tornado hit that afternoon, and we had to postpone it until this coming Saturday."

"You want me to go to the festival with Patrick?"

"Better than that." She tugged her mouth into a sheepish, lopsided grin. "I'd like you two to help me set up and run a booth. I have to decorate, oversee all the activities and clean up afterward. I could use all the extra help I can get."

Peter did a quick mental check of his schedule. He'd have to rearrange a few things, but he could clear his calendar for next Saturday. "Done. We'll be there whenever you need us and stay until the last corn-dog stick is thrown away."

Her smile brightened. "Thank you. And did Patrick mention the Parents' Day Thanksgiving luncheon?"

"I think he gave me a note about that. The day before they get out for Thanksgiving break, right?"

She nodded. "I know it's a work day for most parents, but if you can get there—"

"Say no more. I'll do everything I can to be there. Can my mom come? I know she'd love it."

"By all means. Grandparents are welcome." Her expression darkened slightly, and her brow furrowed. "Peter, how much does Patrick know about his mother?"

Peter's gut pitched and for a moment he couldn't draw a breath. "I…told him the truth. That she died when he was born. Why?"

"That's all you've told him? You don't talk about what

kind of person she was or memories you have of her that he'd find funny or comforting?"

A fist squeezed Peter's heart and filled his chest with an ache that made it difficult to talk. "I don't...I mean...if he asks, I try to...be honest, but..." Peter closed his eyes and gritted his teeth, forcing down the surge of emotion Lisa's question brought.

Katie was the last person he wanted to talk about, but knowing Lisa had bared her soul to him concerning her infertility, he owed her a similar honesty. With a deep breath for courage, he faced his demon.

Chapter 7

"We don't talk about Patrick's mother much. Partly because he doesn't ask, and partly because…well, it's difficult for me. Still."

Lisa reached across the table to touch his hand, her eyes soft with sympathy. "I don't mean to cause you pain, but I think it is important that Patrick know about his mom. Even if he doesn't ask, he's bound to have questions. Not having a mom makes him different from the other kids in his class, and while you've done a commendable job raising him alone—"

"My mother helped a lot. Especially when Patrick was a baby."

She conceded the point with a turn of her hand. "Just the same, a grandmother isn't the same thing as a mom. My last piece of advice—" she quirked a self-conscious grin "—and then I promise not to offer anymore unsolicited opinions—Have a heart to heart with Patrick about your wife. He needs to know who he is, where he came from, what she was like. That she'd have loved him had she lived."

That she'd have loved him. Just when he thought he'd gotten his volatile feelings regarding Katie under control, Lisa's words sucker-punched him. His breath stuck in his lungs. A wave of grief and loss swept through him, shaking him to his marrow. Maybe he wasn't as over Katie's death as he'd thought, if one statement from Lisa could undo him so completely.

Peter fisted his hands and struggled to recover his composure. He nodded when his voice failed him, but finally managed to croak, "I'll keep that in mind."

When she withdrew her hand and resumed eating, Peter regretted the loss of her comforting touch. She clearly sensed she'd broached a sensitive subject and deftly turned the conversation toward more benign topics. Local sports, favorite restaurants, their shared interest in old movies. They chatted amiably through the rest of dinner, then split a decadent chocolate dessert. Peter found a rapport with Patrick's teacher that both put him at ease and filled him with the excitement of a promising new relationship.

He couldn't explain why Lisa Navarre had gotten under his skin when no other woman since Katie had, but the truth was unavoidable. Lisa challenged him, made him rethink aspects of his life he'd too long taken for granted. She reached deep into his soul with her honesty, her warmth, her understanding. Her beautiful smile and womanly curves woke a desire in him he'd denied for a long time.

Yet… *I don't date.*

If losing Katie still hurt after ten years, he couldn't imagine how much pain he'd suffer if he fell in love with Lisa, just to have her walk away. But Lisa had her own demons to battle, and Peter respected her honesty about her past, her reasons not to date.

After the waiter took their plates and left to get their bill, Peter leaned back in the booth and cocked his head. "You know what I wonder?"

Lisa wiped her mouth and sat back with a satisfied sigh. "What?" she asked, grinning.

"If we'd met years ago, before either of us married, before any of the mess we're both dealing with now ever happened…"

Her expression sobered, grew pensive, wistful. "Would we have had the same connection then that we have now?" she finished for him.

So she felt the bond, the magnetic attraction, too? Peter's spirits lifted…until he remembered the obstacles they faced.

Her infertility issues. His gnawing grief over Katie's death. The unsolved attacks on his family.

He flashed a small smile. "Yeah, that."

She held his gaze with eyes full of regret and longing, and a ripple of warmth tripped down his spine. "I guess we'll never know."

On Sunday, Peter took Lisa's advice and made a point of spending time with Patrick—making pancakes together in the morning, tossing the football in the back yard, helping him finish an essay and poster on the Boston Tea Party for school. Working with Patrick on his homework brought thoughts of his dinner with Lisa to mind. While they hadn't gotten the payoff tip from Tess Cantrell that he'd hoped would help find his father's murderer, his non-date with Lisa had been better than expected. He'd gotten an intimate glimpse of the woman who'd captured his attention as well as valuable insights to his relationship with Patrick. All of which served to make Lisa even more enticing, more intriguing and more desirable to him. He found himself restlessly anticipating the school's Fall Festival on Saturday, his next best chance to see Lisa and get to know her.

On Sunday evening as he said goodnight to Patrick, Peter sat on the edge of his son's bed and broached the topic he'd avoided for years. "Patrick, do you have questions about your mom that you want to ask me?"

Patrick's eyes widened, clearly surprised that his father had raised what was usually a taboo topic. "Well...yeah."

He nodded and squeezed Patrick's foot through the covers. "So let's talk. What do you want to know?"

His son swallowed hard and wrinkled his nose reluctantly. "Um...how did she die?"

Peter inhaled deeply, determined to keep his voice steady and reassuring. "There were...complications when you were born. Internal bleeding that the doctor's couldn't stop."

"Oh. Do you miss her?"

Peter squeezed the sports-print bedspread in his hands. "Every day. I wish you could have known her. She was terrific. Really fun, creative, loved to laugh."

Patrick's cheek twitched in a quick grin before sobering. His gaze dropped, and he stared at his hands.

"What is it, Patrick? You can talk to me about it. About anything."

"Do you..." Patrick gulped a deep breath. "Do you blame me for her dying?"

Peter's heart jolted. "What? No!"

Patrick's chin quivered, and Peter felt himself starting to unravel. He scooped his son into a bear hug and crushed him to his chest. "No way, sport. Not one bit. I love you, and I thank God for you every day. Don't ever forget that."

"But she died because of me." Patrick muttered, his voice tight with tears.

"No, she died because her iron was too low and they couldn't stop the bleeding. That's not your fault. No one blames you. No one. Especially not me."

Patrick shuddered and sniffled, and Peter kissed his son on the top of his head. "What's more…" He paused to gather his composure before finishing. "Your mom would have loved you as much as I do. More even. I have no doubt she is looking down from heaven and smiling because she is so proud of you."

"Really?"

"Really."

Patrick wiggled free of Peter's embrace and wiped his face on his pajama sleeve. "Dad, are you dating Ms. Navarre?"

Peter leaned back to get a better view of his son's face. "Would it bother you if I was?"

Patrick groaned. "You're not supposed to answer a question with a question!"

He grinned. "You're right. And no, I'm not dating her. We had dinner the other night, but it was strictly business."

"Business? With my teacher?" Patrick narrowed a skeptical glare on him. "Does that mean you were talking about me?"

"Part of the time. But she also helped interview someone for a case and dinner was my thank-you to her." That much was mostly true.

But Peter heard Lisa's voice in his head, urging him to be completely honest with Patrick.

"But, uh… I do like Ms. Navarre."

Patrick tipped his head. "Just like, or *like* like?"

Peter chuckled. "I think she's pretty and very nice, and

I'd like to see her some more, be her friend. Would that bother you?"

Patrick's grin spread. "That'd be okay. You can even date her if you want. I like her, too."

Peter laughed. "Well, thanks. It's good to have your permission."

Patrick slid back down in his covers with a shrug, missing Peter's sarcasm. "No problem."

Ruffling his son's hair, Peter rose from the bed and snapped off the bedside lamp. "Night, sport. Sleep well." He turned at the door and added, "And anytime you want to talk about Mom or school or anything, you can come to me. Okay?"

"Okay. 'Night, Dad."

Peter headed back to the living room, where he logged onto his computer to catch up on email correspondence and research for a couple cases he had pending. He was at the Montana state records website searching for documents regarding a client's recent divorce when it occurred to him that he could look up May Masterson's and Jeremy Colton's birth certificates to see exactly when the young teens were born and if either certificate listed Mark Walsh as the father. His internet search led him to the usual red tape, but Peter hadn't been a private investigator for seven years without learning a few tricks to get what he needed. A copy of the kids' birth certificates should be on file with their official school records. If he could find a way to steal a peek…

Thoughts of the local schools brought him back to his dinner with Lisa. The pain in her eyes when she'd described her heartache over her broken marriage and her inability to have children gnawed at him. He couldn't imagine his life without Patrick, and if he was honest, he'd always imagined that someday he'd have more kids. He'd come from a large family and wanted Patrick to know the joys of brothers and sisters.

But having more kids meant remarrying. Remarrying meant putting his heart on the line again. Getting involved with a woman meant he must overcome the icy ache deep in his bones when he remembered losing Katie. If he hadn't been able to move past his loss in ten years, what chance did he have of ever putting his wife's death behind him?

And yet…for a few hours Saturday night, Lisa had made him feel as if a future relationship might be possible. The chemistry was definitely there. He'd seen the same attraction burning in her gaze that had sizzled through him when they touched.

I can't put myself through the heartache of another childless relationship.

Peter sighed and rubbed his eyes. He couldn't push Lisa into a relationship she didn't want, and belaboring the point tonight wouldn't help him. He was better off concentrating on his caseload. And on his promise to Craig to find the link between the poisoning and his father's murder.

Setting aside his circular thoughts concerning Lisa Navarre, Peter typed *arsenic sources* into the search engine and looked for something that he could use to prove the Coltons supplied Lester Atkins with the poison used to make Craig sick. Most of what he found he already knew—arsenic is used to make insecticides, fungicides and rodent killer, all of which could have been purchased in bulk from one of the many farm- and ranch-supply stores in the area. While the Coltons had access to these poisons, so did everyone else. Peter raised an eyebrow when he read that a large number of commercially raised chickens were fed a compound containing arsenic. He dismissed this as the source of Craig's illness. Plenty of people ate chicken and didn't wind up in the hospital from it. Craig's poisoning had been deliberate and heavy-handed, intended to kill him.

By midnight, Peter's vision was blurring from reading the small print of the web pages he'd searched and he hadn't learned anything significant to help track down his father's killer.

Shutting down his computer, he decided to pursue the trail of his father's romantic liaisons in the morning. Perhaps someone in town could confirm whether Mark Walsh had gotten involved with Maisie Colton or Lily Masterson fifteen years ago.

As he turned off the lights and headed to bed, Peter recalled his trip to the library last weekend and Maisie's tirade.

Your father sure didn't care how many women he hurt, how many hearts he broke, how many lives he ruined! Did that number include Maisie?

Peter frowned as he climbed into bed. "Guess it is true—Hell hath no fury like a woman scorned."

But had his father's scorn driven one of his women to murder?

The following week dragged for Peter. His cases felt more tedious than usual, and his attention drifted frequently to the unresolved murder of his father. By itself, his father's murder would only be a general concern of wanting justice for his family. But the mounting evidence that Mark Walsh's death had only been the first attack of many directed at his family made finding the person responsible an urgent matter for Peter, a sentiment Sheriff Colton didn't seem to share.

He made a few casual inquiries around town with trusted

friends regarding the possibility that his dad could have had a brief, contentious affair in 1995 with either Lily Masterson or Maisie Colton. His straw poll overwhelmingly favored Lily Masterson as the most likely candidate.

"Face it, Peter. Lily earned the reputation she had back then. She was a wildcat," his barber said as he trimmed Peter's hair. "And Maisie? Well, the way she's storming around town, complaining to anyone who'll listen about the *Dr. Sophie* show not taking her calls, tells me she's not involved with what happened to your dad. Why would she want to go on national TV and draw attention to herself if she were guilty? Don't make sense."

Peter scoffed. "Not much about Maisie Colton makes sense. Besides, have you seen Dr. Sophie's show? Everyone who gets on there is airing their dirty laundry for fifteen minutes of fame."

He was still musing over his barber's comments, though, when he met his mother for lunch the next day at the Honey-B Café on Main Street. Jolene kissed his cheek before she settled in the booth across from him.

"Craig says hello. He's feeling better every day. Stronger."

Peter nodded. "Good. I plan on stopping by to see him later today. I haven't made much progress connecting his poisoning to Dad's murder or the attack on Mary, though."

"Whoever did this had plenty of help. Or they had lots of time to plan and hide themselves under layers of false leads. Like Lester Atkins. Atkins may have had his own reasons to poison Craig, but I'm not convinced he acted alone. But why our family? What do they have to gain by attacking us?" Jolene rubbed the joints of her hand where the earliest stages of arthritis often gave her trouble. "Did you talk to Tess Cantrell?"

"I did."

"And?"

Peter filled his mother in on the conversation with Tess about the volatile woman from Honey Creek Tess had mentioned. Jolene blanched and pressed a hand to her throat when Peter mentioned the mystery woman's pregnancy.

"I'm sorry. I shouldn't have brought that up."

Jolene waved him off. "Please. I'm past the days where your father's sins can hurt me anymore. I'm just startled. That's all. Something that big would be hard to keep a secret." She paused and tapped her fingernails on her coffee mug. "Unless…"

Peter leaned forward. "Yeah?"

"Well, in my day, when a girl got pregnant out of wedlock, the family sent her away to stay with family or stay at a special home for young mothers until the baby came. Maybe this girl left town."

Peter picked up his sandwich, took a big bite and chewed slowly as he thought. "Lily Masterson left Honey Creek back then."

"Hmm…yes. But so did Maisie."

Peter froze. "She did?"

Jolene's gaze drifted away as she tried to recall the specifics. "I think it was just before your dad disappeared. Or was it after? I know it was around then…."

Peter flashed to the newspaper columns he'd scanned through at the library concerning the Coltons. One of the headlines had been about Maisie taking an extended vacation. Ice seeped through his veins.

"Could it have been Maisie Colton, Mom? Could Dad have had a secret affair with the Colton princess and gotten her pregnant? I thought Dad hated the Coltons. All of them."

"It is certainly possible. And if he did, and if Darius

found out Mark had gotten his daughter pregnant? Well…" Jolene tipped her head, her eyebrows lifted, as if to say, "You fill in the blanks."

"Wouldn't have to have been Darius. Her brothers might not have taken too kindly to someone Dad's age messing with their sister. Don't think I haven't noticed Craig's poisoning and the attack on Mary both happened right after Damien was released from prison. Don't you think he's got a grudge to settle with us?" Peter fisted his hand and banged it on the table. "So once again we're back to the Coltons. They seem to be the center of everything in this investigation."

Jolene furrowed her brow and fiddled with her coffee mug. "I know it seems that way to you, but I still think you're focusing on them for personal reasons. Your dad was involved with plenty of other people through his business, his civic groups…his affairs." Jolene splayed her hand on the tabletop and leaned toward Peter. "Honey, I'm worried about you digging into this too deeply. I know you're trying to help Craig find the person who poisoned him, and tie it all to a bigger conspiracy but…I talked to Mary on Sunday and—"

Peter grunted and looked away. "I know where this is going."

"Peter, your sister's life was threatened when she and Jake dug into your dad's business. She's worried about you, worried you'll provoke the wrong people and get hurt. And frankly, I'm worried too. Maybe the time has come to let the matter go and—"

"I can't do that, Mom. Someone is coming after my family. Dad, then Mary, then Craig…I can't sit back and do nothing." Peter tossed enough money on the table to cover their tab and a generous tip. "I have to go. I'm testifying in a personal-injury lawsuit for a client this afternoon. And if I finish at court early enough, I'm going to try to track down proof that Dad is the father of Maisie Colton's son, Jeremy. I know a Colton killed Dad. I just have to figure out which Colton."

Chapter 8

By Thursday afternoon, Peter had grown restless. He was tired of waiting for Saturday to arrive so he could see Lisa at the school's Fall Festival.

As he drove home from Billings, where he'd met with a new client regarding a private search for the woman's missing adult daughter, he had time to think. Two topics stuck center-most in his mind. The questions that still swirled around the attacks on his family...and Lisa Navarre. He couldn't do much more today to resolve the former, but seeing the damage to the trees and buildings on the outskirts of Honey Creek as he pulled back into town reminded him of his promise to fix Lisa's house.

Peter flipped his wrist to check his watch. School would be dismissing in ten minutes. He could pick Patrick up, stop by the hardware store and be at Lisa's house by four o'clock. He'd have about an hour of daylight to replace the roof shingles. A spotlight would be sufficient light to replace her broken window.

His anticipation ramped up as he headed for the elementary school. Once in the carpool line, Peter phoned his mother to let her know her babysitting services were not needed that afternoon. When the last bell rang and kids disgorged from the school, Peter stood beside his truck and scanned the mob of children for Patrick's blue coat and red knit hat. When his son scurried past him, making a beeline for the bus, Peter placed his finger and thumb in his mouth and whistled loudly. "Patrick!"

Stumbling to a stop, Patrick turned toward his father, then trotted over. Instead of the excitement of surprise Peter expected to see, Patrick's face was pale and wary as he approached.

"Dad, wh-what are you doing here?"

"Do I need a reason to pick you up?" Peter put a hand on Patrick's back and ushered him to the passenger's side.

"Is something wrong? Did something else bad happen?" Patrick's voice cracked.

Peter's breath caught. He mentally replayed the past several months, realizing the only times he'd picked Patrick up from school had been when Craig had been poisoned and when Mary had been attacked. "I...no. Nothing bad has happened, sport. I promise. I was just on my way into town from a business trip, and I thought we'd stop by the hardware store together then head over to Ms. Navarre's house to help her with some repairs." He took Patrick's backpack from him as his son climbed onto the front seat. "Does that sound okay to you? I can call Grandma back if you'd rather go home."

Patrick gave him a leery look. "You're sure nothing's wrong? I'm not in trouble?"

Peter smiled and hoisted his son's backpack into the back of the truck. "I'm sure."

But Patrick's wary concern niggled Peter all the way to the hardware store. He recalled Lisa's advice about being honest with his son about all the trouble the family had endured. After they bought the supplies they'd need, he headed to Lisa's house and searched for an opening to discuss the recent family crises with Patrick.

"Sorry I worried you this afternoon, buddy. I didn't realize I'd only picked you up from school on days when there was bad news for the family."

Patrick shrugged. "Whatever."

"Can we talk about what's bothering you?"

"I'm okay."

Peter patted Patrick on the leg. "I know I haven't told you much about what happened to Uncle Craig and Aunt Mary, but that was only because I didn't want to worry you. But I guess not knowing what happened can be just as bad, huh? Not knowing is scary, too."

Patrick glanced at his father with hooded eyes. "I'm not a baby, Dad. You can tell me the truth without me going ballistic."

He smiled at his son. "You're right. You're not a baby. So here's the deal…" Peter explained to Patrick in broad, general terms all that had been transpiring in recent months, careful to reassure him that he had nothing to fear. "The guy responsible for making Uncle Craig sick has been caught and Aunt Mary has given up her investigation of Grandpa's death, so there's nothing to worry about. Right?"

Patrick scrunched his face in thought. "Sorta. Are you investigating Grandpa's death?"

Whoops.

Be honest, he imagined Lisa telling him.

"Well, I'm looking into a few things that might help the sheriff find the person who killed Grandpa. But I'm a professional investigator. I know what I'm doing and how to be careful."

His son scowled. "Why does the sheriff need help? Doesn't he have deputies to help him solve murders?"

Peter squeezed the steering wheel. He hadn't anticipated these landmine questions. "Well, the sheriff didn't ask for my help. I'm doing this on my own. Because I want Grandpa's killer caught as soon as possible."

Patrick turned on the seat, his eyes wide and incisive. "But if Aunt Mary was attacked because she was trying to find out about Grandpa's killer, couldn't they come after you now that you're investigating?"

"I suppose there's a chance. But I'm being very careful." They stopped at a traffic light, and Peter reached over to catch Patrick's chin in his hand. He held his son's face and met his eyes squarely. "Listen to me, Patrick. If I get a sense that I'm in danger, I will quit my investigation without a second thought. Because being here for you and taking care of our family is what is most important to me. I will *not* let anyone hurt me, and more importantly, I will not let anyone hurt you. Ever. Okay?"

Patrick's throat worked as he swallowed. "Promise?"

Peter smiled. "Promise."

"Okay." Patrick returned, grinning. "So can I help fix Ms. Navarre's house?"

Peter released the breath he hadn't realized he'd been holding. "You bet, sport."

"I'm home, Samson!" Lisa called as she hustled in from the cold and left her bag of books by the front door. As she'd left school, she'd have sworn she saw Peter Walsh picking up Patrick, and the handsome father had preoccupied her thoughts ever since. Of course, Peter hadn't been far from her mind all week. When she thought about the Fall Festival and his promise to help set up and work the event, anxious butterflies swooped in her gut. Despite telling herself to take it slow with Peter, to remember her rule about not dating, she couldn't deny the smile that came to her face when she thought of him or the giddy rush of excitement when she looked forward to spending more time with him at the festival.

"Samson?" She shucked off her gloves and scarf and glanced down the hall. Her furry companion emerged from a back room, gave a lazy stretch, then loped with a kind of trot/hop down the hall to greet her. When she reached down to pat him, Samson gave her a cursory rub then headed over to his food bowl. He glared at her as if to say, "It's about time you got home. I'm starving!"

"Yeah, yeah. Let me hang up my coat."

Lisa had just finished feeding Samson, fixing herself a cup of hot tea and settling in her living room with a stack of papers to grade when someone knocked on her front door.

"Who in the world...?" she asked her cat, as he hopped in from the kitchen ready for a post-dinner nap.

She hurried to the door and yanked it open. When she found Peter on her doorstep, his cheeks ruddy from the cold and his jaw shaded with late-afternoon stubble, Lisa's heartbeat scampered.

"Peter." She hoped the breathless quality of her voice sounded more like surprise to him than the girlish giddiness that was, in fact, at fault. She gripped the edge of her door and collected her composure. *Steady, girl*.

"Hi, Ms. Navarre!" Patrick said brightly.

Caught staring at his father, she jerked her gaze to

Patrick and smiled warmly. "Hi, Patrick. What brings you by?"

Patrick held up the toolbox he carried. "We're gonna fix your house."

She glanced back at Peter for confirmation, and he gave her a lopsided grin that did little to help the breathless feeling squeezing her chest. He plucked the toolbox from Patrick's hand and ruffled his son's hair. "Correction. I'm going to fix her roof while you do your homework, and once you finish your schoolwork, you can help me with the window. But homework comes first."

Lisa gave him a sassy grin. "You're just saying that to impress the teacher."

Arching an eyebrow, he replied, "Maybe. Is it working?"

Her smile spread, and she had a playful retort poised on her lips when she caught the fascinated look her student was dividing between her and his father. "Patrick, you can use my kitchen table to do your homework if you want. And help yourself to one of the cookies on the counter if you're hungry."

"Thanks, Ms. Navarre." Patrick plowed through the door with his overstuffed backpack, jostling her into his father's chest as he bustled into her house.

Lisa turned to Peter. "You really don't have to—"

He touched a finger to her mouth to silence her. "But I want to."

The brush of his cold skin on her lips sent sweet sensations curling through her.

"How was I supposed to get any sleep tonight with that arctic front moving in and knowing your window is still broken?"

She hiccupped a laugh. "I don't know. I guess I'll have to let you fix it. We can't have you losing sleep."

An image of Peter, shirtless, restless and tangled in his sheets flashed in her mind, wiping the teasing grin from her face and overloading her circuits.

"I hope you don't mind me bringing him along?" Peter hitched his head toward her kitchen as he stepped inside. "My mom usually keeps him for me in the afternoon, but I thought I'd give her a day off."

Lisa had to swallow before she could speak, the image of Peter in his bed imprinted like a film negative in her brain. "It's fine. He won't bother me. I was just about to grade the history essays they turned in today." She rubbed her palms on the seat of her jeans. "Can I offer you anything before you get started?" *Like permission to have your way with me.*

Oh, mercy. Lisa shoved the provocative images aside. *What is wrong with you?*

"No, I'm good. I've got everything I need in my truck. In fact, I got the last package of black shingles Cooper's Hardware had in stock. Needless to say, they've had a run on building products lately."

"Well, thank you. I'll repay you for the supplies, of course."

He pulled a face and waved her off. "Forget it. My pleasure." He stepped toward her, and she held her breath. But instead of her, his target was the kitchen doorway. He leaned into the room just far enough to send Patrick a parental look. "You behave yourself for Ms. Navarre, and let her get her work done. Understand, sport?"

"Yep." Patrick returned without looking up.

"Yep, *sir*."

"*Sir*," Patrick groaned, apparently missing his father's sarcasm.

Peter lingered for another moment, the whisper of a smile on his lips and an affectionate glow in his eyes as he regarded his son. Peter's obvious love for his son nudged the empty ache in her soul for the children she didn't have, and reminded her why she couldn't burden Peter, or any man, with her infertility.

As he turned toward the door, Peter caught her eye. "I'll be on the roof if you need me."

For the next half hour, Lisa tried hard to concentrate on the history essays, but the thudding on her roof was an ever-present reminder of the man doing the repair, the man who made her pulse hammer.

"I can't think about spelling with all that racket," Patrick complained as he sauntered in from the kitchen and flopped on her couch.

"I know what you mean." Lisa set aside the essays and stretched her back.

Patrick cast a curious gaze around her living room, and his gazed stopped when he spotted Samson napping on the rocking chair by her fireplace. His eyes widened. "Is that your cat?" he asked, even as he crossed the room toward the snoozing feline.

Lisa chuckled. "No, it's my pet shark."

Patrick sent her a withering look and a grin as he knelt in front of the rocking chair. "Can I pet her?"

"That's Samson. You may pet *him,* but be warned, he bites."

Patrick stroked Samson's long fur, and the cat raised his head to greet him with a loud, short, *"Rrow."*

Lisa folded her legs under her, watching Patrick pat Samson and awaiting the inevitable.

Sure enough, Samson batted at Patrick's hand, pinned the boy's hand down with his paw, and—

"He's licking me!" Patrick laughed.

"Licking?" Lisa craned her neck for a better look. "Well, I'll be darned."

Peter's son continued playing with her cat, ruffling his fuzzy tummy and chuckling as Samson batted at his hand. After a moment, Lisa shrugged, baffled by Samson's uncharacteristic behavior, and returned her attention to the history essays.

"Hey, he's only got three legs!" Patrick sounded truly dismayed.

She glanced up again and met the boy's curious gaze. "Yep, I don't know what happened to his other foot. He lost a foot somehow before I rescued him as a kitten."

"Can he walk?" Patrick asked, his expression apprehensive as he continued to pat Samson.

"Oh, yeah, he—"

"Ow! He bit me." The startled but humored expression Patrick wore told her he wasn't hurt. Samson, for all his crankiness, never bit hard.

"I told you." Lisa flashed her student a smile. "He's a shark."

Patrick chuckled and reached for Samson again, but the feline decided he was done amusing their guest and hopped down from the rocking chair. The cat ran off toward the kitchen, answering Patrick's question regarding his mobility.

"Did you finish your homework?" she asked. "Remember, we're having a spelling test tomorrow."

Patrick rolled his eyes and sighed dramatically. "No. I still have to do my math. And my grandma usually helps me study spelling."

Lisa set aside the history papers and rose to scoot Patrick back to the kitchen table. "Your dad wants you to finish your schoolwork before you help with the window. If you want me to quiz you in spelling, I can."

Patrick looked up at her, his face brightening. "Really? Can you help me with my math, too?"

"What's your trouble with math? You've been doing well on all your assignments so far this year."

"I just hate fractions is all."

"If you're asking me to do your math for you the answer is no. But if you get stuck, give a holler. Okay?"

"Give a holler?" Patrick laughed. "You sound like a hick."

Lisa pretended to be affronted. "*Holler* is a perfectly good word down in Texas, where I grew up." She propped her hands on her hips and scowled playfully. "And I'm fixin' to open a can of whoop-butt on you if you don't get your hide into the kitchen and get busy."

Though he grinned at her southernisms spoken with a heavy drawl, Patrick's eyes widened, and he jumped up and scurried to the kitchen table. She followed him and paused to tousle his hair.

How many times had she imagined sitting around the table with her own family, sharing meals or tutoring on homework? She suppressed a pang of regret and focused on his cherubic face. In a few years, with the sculpting of maturity, Patrick would be the spitting image of his father.

While Patrick tackled fractions, she started a package of hamburger browning, glancing toward the table every now and then to check on her student. "How's it going?"

"Okay. Just two more to go. Then spelling."

She pulled a jar of spaghetti sauce from the cabinet and turned down the heat on the beef.

As she headed to the table, Patrick closed his math book and sighed. "Why do you give so much homework?"

"Patrick, ten math problems and twenty vocabulary words is not that much homework."

She slid his spelling book toward her and flipped to the right page. "Ready?"

He nodded. "If I get them all right, do I get a dollar?"

She laughed. "If you get them all right tomorrow, you'll get an A on your test."

"Grandma gives me a dollar if I spell all my words right."

"Hmm, well, you can take that up with your dad. For now, spell *abject*."

They made their way through most of the list before Peter sauntered in from outside, bringing the crisp scent of autumn leaves with him.

"Hey Dad, Ms. Navarre has a cool cat named Samson. He's only got three legs, and his fur is really soft. First he was licking me, and then he bit me!"

Peter frowned. "Bit you?"

Lisa opened her mouth to defend her cat, but Patrick rushed on enthusiastically. "Not hard. It didn't hurt. He's really awesome, Dad."

"Awesome? Wow. High praise for a cat." He pulled off his coat and hung it in the front hall. "So how's the homework coming?"

Patrick's shoulders slumped. "I'm still studying spelling for my test."

His dad twisted his mouth in thought. "Tell you what. Do as much as you can while I set things up for the window, then I'll finish quizzing you while we work. Deal?"

"Deal!"

"Peter?" Lisa said impulsively. "I'd love for you to stay and eat with me. I'm making spaghetti. It's the least I can do to say thank you."

"Spaghetti! Can we, Dad? Please?" Patrick's expression was enthusiastic and pleading. Lisa just hoped her own face didn't reflect the same expectant eagerness, despite the thump of adrenaline and hopefulness in her chest.

"You sure you have enough to share? Growing boys eat a lot."

She winked at Patrick. "I'm sure."

Peter's face warmed, and his smile sent a zing through her blood. "Thank you. We accept. Let me go get the new window out of the truck and I'll let you know when I'm ready to start, okay, Patrick?"

As Peter headed out to his truck, Lisa tried to tame the giddy smile that tugged her cheeks.

Patrick would be with them, chaperoning, so her dinner invitation couldn't be considered a date. Right? Repaying his kindness was the least she could do.

So why did having Peter and his son staying for dinner feel like something special, something significant?

Setting aside the nagging questions, she glanced down at Patrick's spelling list. "Okay, spell *dangerous*."

Her pulse stumbled. An omen? Was pursuing this "non-relationship" with Peter a dangerous venture for her heart?

Not a date, she told herself. *It's not a date.*

Peter removed the cardboard Lisa had taped over her broken window and set it aside while the image of his son sitting at the kitchen table with the pretty brunette replayed in his head. Patrick seemed to be gobbling up the female attention. And why not? Lisa was attractive, kind, invested in seeing Patrick do well in school. Had he underestimated the importance of having a mother figure in his son's life?

Sure, his mom was there for Patrick every afternoon, but somehow that was different. Jolene was Patrick's grandmother, only available part-time. A whole generation older than Patrick's friends' mothers.

Lisa would make a great mother. As soon as the thought

filtered through his head, he remembered her painful confession at the restaurant on Saturday. A fist of regret squeezed his chest. Not only did her infertility troubles make her gun-shy about dating, reluctant to risk the kind of pain she'd known with her ex-husband, but she was missing out on one of life's truly great joys. Parenting Patrick filled his heart in unexpected and powerful ways.

When he and Katie had been anticipating Patrick's birth, they'd talked about how many more children they'd have.

Twelve, Katie had said, *just like in* Cheaper by the Dozen.

Peter had laughed and kissed his wife. *Let's see how this first one goes before we commit to a dozen.*

He sighed as the tightness in his chest gripped harder. Katie hadn't lived long enough even to see Patrick grow up. And deep inside he still harbored a desire for more kids. Maybe not twelve, but…

Peter removed the wrappings from the new window and was lining up the needed tools when Patrick bustled into the room. "Ms. Navarre says to let her know when to start the noodles. They take about ten minutes to boil."

Shaking off the melancholy that thoughts of Lisa's infertility and Katie's death had stirred, he managed a smile for his son. "Copy that. So did you bring your spelling words?"

Patrick handed him a thin book. "Page 44. We stopped at *extensive*."

Flipping to the proper page, Peter scanned the list and read aloud, *"Exude."*

"Exude. E-x-u—" Patrick paused and took the screwdriver Peter handed him. "—d-e. *Exude.*"

Peter pointed to a screw on the existing window frame. "See if you can remove that screw, then tell me what *exude* means."

Patrick set to work on the screw. "We don't have to know the definitions for the test. Just spell the words."

"Yeah, maybe so. But *I* want you to tell me what the words mean while we work."

His son groaned. "*Exude* means...like...stuff coming out or oozing from something?"

"Basically, yeah." He watched Patrick struggle to loosen the screw. "Can you use it in a sentence?"

Another grunt. "Dad!"

"Patrick!" he returned mimicking his son's exasperated tone.

His son bit his bottom lip and leaned into his efforts to budge the stuck screw. When it turned, Patrick's face lit with victory. "Did it."

"Excellent." He gave his son's upper arm a light squeeze. "Yep, definitely getting some muscles there. Now... *exude*."

Patrick tipped his head and wrinkled his nose. Then a sassy grin lit his face. "Ms. Navarre's cat exudes awesomeness."

A chuckle behind them drew his attention to the door. Lisa leaned against the frame watching them, looking beautiful with a mysterious little smile tugging her lips.

Peter's pulse kicked as the impulse to taste those lips slammed into him.

"Works for me, Dad. Although I'm not sure if *awesomeness* is in the dictionary," she said.

Patrick nudged Peter out of the way, pulling his dad from his lustful sidetrack, and set to work loosening the next screw holding the broken window in place. "Dad, can we get a cat?"

Peter pulled a dubious frown. "A cat? Wouldn't a dog be more...a guy's pet?"

Patrick shrugged. "I don't know. I like Samson. I want a cat like him."

Peter sent Lisa a look and caught her smirking, muffling a laugh. "Yeah, well…we'll see. I'm not much of a cat person."

Over the next twenty minutes, Patrick loosened all of the remaining screws and helped him lift down and replace the broken window. Lisa checked on them several times, complimenting Patrick on his handyman skills and smiling her approval to Peter. When they had secured the new window and sealed the edges with caulk, he cast a glance over his shoulder to Lisa. "All done here. Just need to clean up, if you want to start the pasta."

"Got it." She pushed away from the wall where she'd been leaning and stepped closer to examine their work. "Double-paned for extra insulation, even. Wow."

Peter handed his son a small bag of trash. "Please take this to her garbage can outside."

When Patrick reached for the old window, Peter and Lisa spoke at the same time.

"Wait!"

"Patrick, don't—"

He looked up at them, confused.

"Let me get the broken glass, sport. I don't want you to cut yourself." Peter ruffled Patrick's hair. "Take that trash out, then wash up for dinner."

After Patrick left, Lisa sidled closer to Patrick and pitched her voice low. The scent of her perfume teased his nose and made his body go haywire.

"You're good with him. Patient. Firm but loving. Instructing without being bossy or demeaning. I know I have no room to judge since I'm not a parent myself—"

"Lisa—" He furrowed his brow, sensing where this might be going.

She raised a finger to stop him.

"And it really isn't my business anyway, but…in case there is any question left about my opinion of the job you're doing with Patrick—" she flashed a gentle smile "—you're a great father. I can see how much you love him in the way you look at him."

He nodded. "He's everything to me."

A wistful look drifted over her face, and she turned back to the new window, ran her fingers over the glass. "It looks like a professional did this. Thank you, Peter." She lifted a corner of her mouth, an impish light sparking in her eyes as she nudged him with her shoulder. "And for the record, the teacher *is* impressed."

"I'm glad." The temptation to kiss her sucker-punched him again, making his body taut, as if his skin were too tight. He canted slightly forward, his gaze locked on hers.

And Patrick barreled back into the room, the bag of trash still in his hand. "It's too dark outside."

Peter jerked away from his son's teacher and cleared his throat. "What?"

"I can't see anything. Can you turn on a light for me?"

Lisa's expression reflected the same crushed anticipation as she ushered Patrick into the hall. She met his gaze as she left the room, her eyes full of the same regret that hammered him.

Trying not to resent the missed opportunity to sample her lips, Peter carefully picked up the broken window and followed them down the hall. Somehow, some way, he'd find another chance to show Lisa Navarre how he felt about her.

Chapter 9

Saturday morning, Peter and Patrick rose early and headed over to the school gymnasium to help Lisa decorate and set up for the Fall Festival. They arrived just as Lisa was unloading a large box from the back of her car, and Peter swooped in to take the box from her.

"I'll get that."

"Morning, Ms. Navarre!" Patrick said, a bounce of preteen energy in his step.

"Hi, guys!" Her face brightened as she passed the bulky load to Peter. "You came."

"Didn't I say we would?"

"Well, yeah, but...I guess I didn't expect you until later." She nodded to the box as she started for the gym door. "Looks like you arrived right on time, though. Thank you."

He flashed a broad grin. "I aim to please."

Patrick held the door as Peter carried the large box

inside and set it on a folding table near the door. A few other parents and teachers already milled about in the gym, hanging posters, unfolding chairs and shuffling volleyball nets off the main floor. Peter scanned the faces, recognizing a few. No Coltons.

He hoped to have a chance to question some of the other parents, and get a feel for what the local grapevine was saying about his dad's death. The Honey Creek gossip mill had an uncanny way of learning who did what long before official channels did.

"What is all this stuff?" Patrick asked, peering into the box.

Lisa started unpacking papers, baskets, balls, staplers, scissors and rolls of tape. "Decorating supplies. Odds and ends for the games." She handed Patrick three small rubber balls. "Will you take these to Mrs. Jones for the milk-can-toss booth?"

"Sure."

While his son scurried away with the rubber balls, Peter stepped closer to Lisa, mindful of the eyes watching him and the pretty teacher. "How is it you look so pretty at this hour on a Saturday morning?"

She gave him choked-sounding chuckle. "What? Are you kidding? No makeup, faded jeans and a ratty ponytail? Who are you kidding?"

He turned up a palm. "I just call 'em as I see 'em."

Patrick returned, gushing with the eagerness of a puppy. "Now what?"

"Well, will you help me make copies of these coloring sheets for the little kids?" Lisa pulled a couple of pages with black line drawings from a folder and held them out to Patrick.

"Okay. What do I do?"

"Follow me to the front office, and I'll show you how

to work the copy machine." After popping a few pieces of candy corn in her mouth, she pulled out a wad of keys and jangled them as she hitched her head, signaling Patrick to follow her.

The front office. Peter stilled. This could be his opportunity to get the information he needed on Maisie Colton's son.

"Hey, Patrick?" he called, trotting to catch up. "Why don't you help Mrs. Robbins set up chairs? I'll make the copies with Ms. Navarre."

Patrick divided a curious look between Lisa and his father. "You just want privacy so you can kiss, don't you?"

Lisa sputtered a laugh, her cheeks flushing. "Patrick!"

"None of your beeswax, sport. Now go help with the chairs." Peter took the coloring sheets from Patrick, curled them into a cone and swatted at his son's fanny as Patrick loped away, smirking.

Facing Lisa, Peter rolled his eyes. "Sorry about that. The boy never did miss a chance to embarrass his old man."

Lisa bumped him with her shoulder as they started down the corridor. "Not so old."

Peter gave her an appreciative grin. "Most men my age are only just now starting to have babies. When most guys were graduating from college and thinking about marriage, I was parenting a toddler. Alone."

Lisa grew quiet, pensive. He could guess where her mind was. *Stupid, stupid, bring up babies!*

"Sorry—" he said at the same time she started, "Peter, do you ever—"

He waved a hand. "Go on."

"Do you think about having more kids?"

He sighed. "The thought has crossed my mind. I came from a relatively large family. I enjoyed having a brother and two sisters to play with growing up. I'd love for Patrick to have that, but at this point he's already got a ten-year head start on any siblings he'd have, so they wouldn't exactly be contemporaries."

"But you do want more kids?"

They stopped in front of the front office, and when she reached for the knob to unlock the door, he caught her hand. "I know where this is coming from. I shouldn't have mentioned kids around you. I'm sorry."

Her eyes lit with a fiery intensity. "Wrong. The last thing I want you to do is dance around subjects with me. Especially when it comes to children. If we're going to see more of each other, then it's something we have to deal with up front."

He drew her closer, and her eyes widened with surprise. "*Are* we going to see more of each other?"

"I…I only meant—"

"Because I'd like that. A lot."

"I—" She licked her lips and cast her gaze toward his chest. "Peter, I like you. Really I do, but what's the point in dating if—"

He caught her chin and nudged her face up. "Here's the point."

Without a second thought, he dipped his head and caught her lips with his, shaping and molding them with a gentle persuasion.

Lisa stiffened in shock, then slowly melted into his embrace, answering the tug of his mouth with a reciprocal fervor. Her kiss tasted like the candy corn she'd been nibbling, and like a sugar rush in his blood, the sweet pressure of her lips made his pulse pound and wired his body with a surge of energy.

The clang of a locker closing down the hall startled them, and Lisa jerked back from his arms. Touching her lips, she glanced up from hooded eyes and sent him a devilish grin. "Are you trying to get me in trouble with the principal, sir?"

"Certainly not. But Patrick put the idea in my head, and…well, it was a good idea, so…"

She blushed a darker pink and turned to unlock the door. "The copier is in the far corner over there." She pointed out the device to Peter, then turned the thumb lock on the door. "Pull the door closed when you leave. It should lock."

"You're leaving?"

"I think you can handle the copier alone. I've got a mess of things still to do. See you back in the gym in a few…"

"Mm-hm," he called to her as she started back down the hall. "You're just scared to be alone with me. Aren't you? You know I'll kiss you again, and you won't want to stop."

She turned, grinning as she put a finger to her lips to shush him.

Peter lingered in the office door, enjoying the sway of her hips as she sashayed down the corridor. Once she disappeared around the corner, Peter crossed the office and powered on the copier. While it warmed up, he glanced around and located a long, low file cabinet with drawers labeled A-F, G-N, O-Z. He tested the top drawer and found it locked. Naturally. Did he really think the school left personal records for the students that vulnerable?

With a quick glance toward the door, Peter pulled out his pocket knife and jimmied the top drawer lock. When it snicked open, he slid the drawer out, flipped through the files until he found Jeremy Colton's, and spread the folder on the desk. He paged through transcripts, noting that Jeremy was a good student and had been given both academic awards and citizenship recognition. He paused to study the most recent school photo, clipped on the inside cover of the file.

Did Jeremy bear any resemblance to the Walshes? Peter's heart clamored in his chest. He imagined that he saw his father in Jeremy's eyes, in his crooked smile, in his chin. With a huff of disgust, Peter turned the page. He was only seeing what he thought he should see. The kid looked like his mother, like a Colton.

At the back of the file, Peter found what he was looking for. A photocopy of Jeremy's birth certificate.

A thump in the hall, followed by the sound of young voices chattering and giggling, called Peter's attention to the corridor.

Hurry.

He scanned the document, noting the date of birth— seven months after his father had disappeared in 1995—and the space for the father's name.

Blank.

Peter suppressed a groan. No help there.

Unless…Maisie had been unwilling to publicly acknowledge the boy's father due to the scandal it could cause.

I mean, big-time scandal and hush-hush. Tess Cantrell's assessment rang in his head, and a chill slithered down Peter's back.

The copier beeped that it was ready, and Peter carried Jeremy's file over, laid out the copy of the birth certificate and Jeremy's photo and pressed Copy. When the machine spat out the pages he wanted, Peter folded them three times and shoved the papers deep in his back pocket for closer inspection later. Returning the evidence to the file, Peter stuck Jeremy's file back behind Collins, Sara, jimmied the lock closed and set to work copying the coloring sheets for the festival.

* * *

Lisa was filling the apple-bobbing tub with water when Peter strolled into the gymnasium. Just the sight of him, his loose-hipped amble, his broad shoulders and form-fitting jeans stirred a restless hunger in her belly. Her lips twitched, remembering the mind-blowing kiss he'd startled her with in the hall.

He flopped the stack of coloring sheets on the table beside her. "Your papers, milady."

She grinned. "Thank you, sir."

He spread his hands. "What should I do next?"

Kiss me again. She bit down on her bottom lip to keep from blurting the reply that sprang to mind. Unlike the deserted hallway, the gymnasium buzzed with activity as more students and parents arrived to set up booths from a cupcake walk to a beanbag toss. Kissing Peter Walsh now would start rumors flying faster than the kamikaze bumblebees that even now were swooping in her stomach. Too bad they'd nixed the idea of a kissing booth when Mrs. Holloway raised her concerns about passing germs.

"You can help me hang the decorations. I have balloons, streamers to go up, and a banner needs to be hung over the main stage."

Peter clapped his hands together. "Great. Let's do it."

She directed him to the stepladder the custodian had left out for their use and collected the decorations that needed to be put up, a stapler, a roll of heavy-duty tape and a hammer.

As Peter brought the ladder over to the corner of the stage where she waited, Patrick ran up to him, followed at a more leisurely pace by Jeremy Colton.

"Dad, Jeremy's mom brought a ton of cupcakes for the cupcake walk, but she said I can have one now if it's okay with you."

Knowing Peter's feelings toward the Coltons, especially his suspicions about Maisie having an affair with his father, Lisa watched Peter's reaction closely. Setting the ladder down, Peter turned to Patrick, then, as if he'd just noticed his son's companion, lifted a sharp gaze to the second boy. He tensed slightly, his expression reflecting surprise, but he quickly schooled his face and sent the boy an awkward grin. "Hello, Jeremy." Then to Patrick, "I didn't know you and Jeremy were friends."

Patrick shrugged. "We ride the same bus, so we talk sometimes. So can I have one of the cupcakes?"

Peter sent his gaze across the room to the table where Maisie Colton was unpacking several bakery boxes and lining up cupcakes on a plate. "I, uh… Isn't it kinda early for sweets?" He checked his watch and sent Patrick a skeptical look.

"Da-ad!" Patrick groaned. "Please? I'm starving."

He sighed. "One. Only one."

"Yeah!" Patrick brightened, exchanged a high five with Jeremy, and loped off to collect his treat.

His hands balled at his sides, Peter watched his son approach Maisie. "What is she doing here? Her kid is in junior high."

"Because our festival was delayed, we combined with the junior high this year." She nudged Peter's shoulder. "You know, I taught Jeremy. He really is a good kid. You don't have to worry about Patrick hanging out with him."

The boys reached the table, spoke to Maisie, and she lifted a startled glance to Peter that morphed into a hostile glare.

"It's not Jeremy that bothers me," he muttered, turning away from Maisie's stare and shifting the ladder closer to where she stood.

"Wow, y'all are regular Hatfields and McCoys. What

started this hatefest anyway? Has your family always had a feud with the Coltons?" She scooted the ladder to where she needed it and handed him the decorations to hold while she climbed up.

He steadied the ladder and tipped his head back to meet her gaze from her perch on the top rung. "Not always. Seems like way back when I was younger, our families might have even been friends. But something happened a long time ago that made my dad really hate the name Colton. I'm not even sure what it was. Probably something business-related. Then when Lucy started dating Damien, the you-know-what really hit the fan. It just escalated from there."

She frowned and held out her hand for the streamers. "What a shame. The two most prominent families in town fighting. Think of all the good you all could do if you spent the same energy doing things to heal the town and help the needy."

Peter's spine stiffened. "The Walshes do tons of good for this town. Besides, do you really expect us to ignore the fact that a Colton was convicted of killing my dad in 1995?"

"He's since been cleared."

"Yeah, yeah. That doesn't erase the ill-will. A Colton could easily be responsible for real this time." Peter's jaw tightened, and he sent a dark look across the room to Maisie.

"Look, I don't mean to preach. I just hate to see you poison the next generation if there is no proof the Coltons are responsible for your family's trouble." She hitched her head to where Jeremy and Patrick stood licking the icing off their cupcakes and laughing together. "They don't have any ill will."

Peter glanced at his son, and his expression softened. "I

have no intention of interfering with my son's friendships. If Jeremy is a good kid, then—"

"He is." She pointed to the stapler. "Will you hand me that?"

Peter picked up the stapler and climbed several rungs to hand it to her.

When the ladder rocked slightly, Lisa gasped and groped for something to hold on to. "Hey, you're supposed to be steadying the ladder!"

He passed the stapler to her and gave her a wolfish grin. "I'd rather steady you." He demonstrated by splaying a wide, warm hand at the base of her spine. "The ladder's stable. Just be sure *you* don't keel over."

I'm more likely to fall off if you keep touching me like that.

Heat from his hand sent a sweet sensation tingling up her back. When he moved up a couple of more rungs, his arms surrounded her as he held on to the ladder, and his body heat wrapped around her like a hug. His freshly-showered scent tickled her nose and made her heart thump a wild cadence.

Her hand trembled from the adrenaline of having him so close, the memory of his seductive kiss still zinging through her. When she tried to staple a banner into place, her reach proved too short, and without her asking, Peter took the banner from her hand and held it in place. On her toes and stretching her arm, she slapped a couple of staples in the sign, then clutched at Peter's arm when the ladder wobbled again.

"I got you," he murmured close to her ear.

With a nervous chuckle, she released his arm. "Yeah, but who's got you? If this ladder tips, we'll both go down."

She started to move down the ladder, but Peter stayed put, putting him at eye level with her once she'd climbed down a couple rungs. She turned in the tight space between his broad chest and the ladder and met the smoky look in his eyes.

"I, uh, need to get some balloons." Her voice cracked, giving away the nervous flutter pinging in her chest.

"I want to see you again." His voice was low and husky, his dark eyes penetrating, smoldering.

Her head spun, and she groped behind her for a rung to cling to. Tugging her lips in a lopsided grin, she said, "You're going to see lots of me today. I'm going to need plenty of help with the booths once the festival opens."

"I want to see you again *alone*." He tucked a wisp of hair that had escaped her ponytail behind her ear, and a thrill raced through her. "Next weekend. Let me take you out to the Walsh family ranch. We can ride the horses out on the property or take the sleigh out and have a picnic."

"A picnic? In November?" She tried to sound lighthearted. A difficult trick considering her breath had lodged in her lungs the instant his bedroom gaze latched onto hers, and his proximity had her heart thundering for all it was worth.

He nodded. "Beside a bonfire. I'll bring blankets and hot coffee." He shrugged and canted closer to her. "Or we can stay in and eat by the fireplace. Your choice."

Lisa cast a glance over his shoulder to the other parents and kids milling about the gymnasium. She could already hear the tongues wagging over the cozy scene between the fourth-grade teacher and one of the fathers. "I…I'd like to but—"

"No buts. It's a date." When she opened her mouth to counter, he pressed his fingers to her lips, and a crackle, like heat lightning, fired from every synapse. "A real date. I know you're worried about getting involved with someone, but I think if we talk about it, we can figure something out."

A bittersweet pain swelled in her chest. She wanted to believe there was hope for her to build a relationship with someone someday. And Peter was certainly the kind of man she could see herself falling for. But the power of her attraction to him also rang warning bells. The harder she fell for him, the more it would hurt if they couldn't find an agreeable compromise about how the relationship would work.

"We can go slow," he said, seeming to read her mind. "But I want—"

"Dad, Jeremy and I are gonna shoot some hoops out on the basketball court, okay?" Patrick called from the foot of the ladder.

Peter jerked away from her and started down the ladder. "What about helping Ms. Navarre set up the booths? That's what we came to do."

Lisa struggled for a breath as she followed Peter down the ladder.

"Aw, Dad..." Patrick frowned and gave his friend a shrug.

"You'll have lots of time for playing later." He handed Patrick a package of balloons. "Why don't you guys blow these up for us? I know you boys are full of hot air, so..."

Jeremy chuckled, and Patrick groaned at Peter's joke.

Feeling much steadier and in control once her feet were again on the ground and Peter's heavenly scent wasn't scrambling her thoughts, Lisa handed Patrick some ribbon. "Once you blow them up, tie them in bunches of three and put them up all around. Tie them to chairs, doors, anywhere you think the place needs sprucing up."

"Okay," the boys answered together before wandering off with their new assignment.

Using the distraction to gather her thoughts, Lisa fumbled with a poster she'd made for the bean-bag-toss booth and kept her gaze on her hands. "Peter, I'm flattered by the invitation. Can I think about it and give you an answer later today?"

When she peeked up at him, he was still watching her with those dark bedroom eyes. She wanted to drown in those eyes, wanted to sink into their depths and forget that Mother Nature had cursed her with fibroids that had prevented her from getting pregnant and had eventually led to her hysterectomy.

"Sure." With a quick smile that said he knew he was being put off, he picked up the ladder and moved it down the stage to tack up the next section of the banner.

Lisa swallowed the lump that rose in her throat. When she'd divorced Ray, she thought she'd endured the most painful effect of her infertility. She hadn't counted on meeting a man like Peter, who made her want to be part of a family all over again.

"Come on, sport, give it your best shot!" Peter called from the dunking booth as Patrick wound up to throw at the target.

Since opening to the community three hours ago, the Fall Festival had been packed with children and their parents. The cheerful fall decor of pumpkins, dried corn stalks and colorful leaf collections gave the school a festive mood, and the scents of fresh popcorn and cotton candy that filled the air brought back memories of summer carnivals Lisa had attended as a child. Without a doubt, the festival had been a smashing success for the PTA.

For Lisa, personally, the day had exceeded her expectations, thanks in large part to the man sitting in the dunking booth and his son, winding up for his pitch.

"You're going down, Dad!" Patrick hurled the tennis ball at the target, hit the bullseye, and Peter splashed down into the water to the cheers of the crowd gathered around the booth.

Lisa saw Peter shiver as he came up from the cold water, although he hadn't complained once. He'd been a good sport about sitting in the dunking booth for almost an hour. "Okay, I think poor Mr. Walsh has had enough. Who is our next volunteer? Principal Green?"

A cheer went up from the gathered kids, who scrambled to be first in line to dunk the principal.

Laughing at the kids' enthusiasm, Lisa walked around to the back of the dunking booth just as Peter was stepping down from the perch and peeling off his sopping T-shirt. Her steps faltered, and she nearly swallowed her tongue.

Peter Walsh's muscled chest and arms, flat stomach and arrow of dark hair that disappeared into his wet jeans were fodder for any woman's most sensual fantasy.

"Can you hand me that towel?" he asked, pointing to the stack of clean towels waiting for the dunkees to dry off.

She had to mentally shake herself from her gaping stupor in order to process his request and respond. "Uh, sure."

Patrick wheeled around the corner of the booth. "Ha! I got you good, huh, Dad?"

"That you did, buddy. Along with several dozen other folks." Peter shook his head like a dog, spraying Patrick and Lisa with droplets of water. Lisa raised the towel she was about to hand Peter as a shield.

"Hey!" Patrick laughed.

Peter tossed his son his keys. "Run out to the truck and bring me the dry clothes in my gym bag, will ya, sport?"

"Sure, Dad."

As Patrick trotted off, Lisa offered Peter the towel. "Thanks for doing that." She hitched her head to the booth where Mr. Green was now taunting the kids trying to dunk him. "I know it was a cold job."

Peter shrugged. "Not too bad. Glad to help. Patrick really seemed to get a kick out of it."

"He wasn't the only one. I think you're lucky Maisie Colton was stopped when she was." She rolled her eyes, thinking of the way Maisie Colton had elbowed people out of the way when Peter climbed in the booth, then spent twenty minutes and fifty dollars throwing balls, trying to soak Peter. Had other parents not intervened and insisted Maisie give someone else a chance, Lisa had no doubt Maisie would have soon started throwing the tennis balls right at Peter's head. Yet Peter had been a good sport, keeping a smile on his face, despite the daggers in Maisie's eyes as she'd dunked him over and again.

"More money for the school. Glad my family's feud with the Coltons proved lucrative for the Festival." He flashed her a wry smile.

When he shivered again, Lisa winced. "Let me buy you a hot chocolate at least. You need something to warm you up."

He stepped closer and arched a dark eyebrow. "I bet a kiss would do the trick."

Her breath caught, and she felt her cheeks heat.

"But I guess there are too many spectators here for that, huh?" His smile was devilish. "I'll take the hot chocolate for now."

With a jerky nod, she hurried off to join the concessions line, winding up behind two women deep in conversation.

"If Maisie Colton doesn't shut up about the *Dr. Sophie* show, I think I'm going to have to shut her up!" The first woman complained loudly to her friend. "I know they say the rich are eccentric, but sometimes I think Maisie takes eccentric to a new level!"

"I know it. Did you see the way she knocked Emily Waters out of the way to be first in line to dunk Peter Walsh? She's an embarrassment to the school."

Lisa looked at her feet, pretending not to listen. But the women didn't seem to care who heard them as they fussed at full volume.

"Did you hear what she said when Mr. Green finally pulled her out of line so the kids could play?"

"No. What?"

"She said, and I quote, 'You Walshes deserve that and more! I thought I was rid of Mark Walsh the first time, but at least he's gone for good this time. He got what he deserved!'"

A chill skittered down Lisa's back.

The other woman gasped. "She did?"

"No lie. The Walsh family is mourning Mark's murder, and she has the nerve to say he got what he deserved." Now the woman did pitch her voice lower. "Although, from what I hear, Mark Walsh was a reprobate who slept with anything in a skirt."

Lisa tensed. Was this the kind of catty gossip Peter had grown up hearing? She glanced across the gymnasium floor in time to see Peter take his gym bag from Patrick and speak to an older woman with red hair as he headed into the locker room to change. The woman gave Patrick a big hug then, when Patrick pointed at Lisa, the woman smiled and waved.

Lisa waved back, then turned to move up in the line and place her order. She carried a tray with four hot chocolates back to where Patrick and the older woman waited for Peter. "Cocoa for everyone!"

"Oh, thank you, honey," the woman said with a smile. "I'm Jolene Walsh. Patrick's grandmother."

And Peter's mother.

Still shaken by the exchange between the gossipy women, Lisa forced a grin and balanced the hot chocolate tray as she offered her hand to Jolene Walsh and introduced herself.

"Thanks, Ms. Navarre. Dad said to tell you he'd be right back." Patrick helped himself to a cup and handed one to his grandmother. "Can we do the cupcake walk again? I'm getting hungry."

"Do it *again?*" Mrs. Walsh asked Patrick. "How many times have you done the cupcake walk?"

He shrugged. "A couple."

Lisa laughed. "You mean a couple of dozen?"

By her count, she, Peter and Patrick had made the rounds of all the games and booths at least eight times, and for Patrick's favorites, like the cupcake walk, the number was much higher.

Jolene gave her grandson a crooked smile. "Tell you what. We'll do the cupcake walk, but if you win the cupcake, you save it for after dinner."

Patrick cocked his head as if considering the deal. "Okay!"

"Want to come?" the redhead asked Lisa.

"No, I'll wait here for Peter," she replied, indicating the hot drink in her hand was for him.

Patrick dragged his grandmother off to the cupcake booth, and Lisa sighed contentedly. The afternoon had passed quickly and been filled with laughter, good-spirited competition between the father and son, and a growing sense of family. Which was ridiculous, because Peter and Patrick weren't her family. Technically, she wasn't even dating Peter. But…

I want to see you again alone.

Heaven help her, she wanted to see Peter again—alone—too. She wanted to explore the familial warmth their time together today had nurtured, wanted to share more steamy kisses like the one Peter had stolen in front of the office, wanted to give Patrick the motherly love and attention a boy his age deserved.

But mostly her day with Peter and Patrick had woken her soul-deep desire for her own child, a yearning that could never be fulfilled. Spending more time with the Walsh family could only exacerbate the painful longing. So why was she actually considering Peter's invitation for another date? A real date. A date that would acknowledge that they shared an electric attraction and had fun together.

And today had been fun. More fun than she'd had in years.

"That for me?"

She startled when Peter's voice broke into her reverie. The hot cocoa sloshed onto her hand, and she gasped.

"Whoa, sorry. Didn't mean to spook you." He took the hot chocolate and flashed a smile that did more to warm her inside than the sweet drink. Peter had changed into dry jeans and a flannel button-down shirt that reminded her of Paul Bunyon, and had combed his wet hair back from his face. With his five o'clock shadow and dark hair peeking from the collar of his shirt, he looked woodsman-rugged and thoroughly sexy.

She was in trouble. She was falling fast and hard for this man and his son. Even as she told herself she should turn and run, she heard herself saying, "Yes, I'd love to see you again next weekend."

Peter blinked as he took a gulp of his cocoa and played mental catch-up to her out-of-context comment. But soon a satisfied grin tugged his cheek and his eyes warmed.

"Great. I'll get my mom to watch Patrick, and we'll have the whole day."

Lisa's stomach flip-flopped with anticipation and giddy delight. A whole day alone with Peter Walsh.

A whole day.

Alone.

With Peter.

What had she done?

Chapter 10

Before the Fall Festival officially wound down, Peter could tell Patrick had reached his limit of fun and frosting and would soon reach critical mass if he didn't go home and decompress. Peter's mother volunteered to take Patrick home so that Peter could stay and help tear down the booths and haul some of the larger materials back to Lisa's house in his truck.

"How did you get this *to* the school?" he asked as they carried a tall plywood backboard for the bean-bag toss out of the gymnasium. "I know this didn't fit in your car."

Lisa puffed a wisp of her dark hair out of her face. "Nope. Harvey brought it over for me in his truck."

"Harvey?" Peter couldn't help the prick of jealousy that poked him at the idea of another man going to Lisa's house, winning one of her bright smiles for his helpfulness.

"Principal Green," Lisa clarified.

Peter pictured the short, aging principal and felt somewhat better. Not that he had any right to feel possessive of Lisa's attention.

"Bye, Ms. Navarre!" a young voice shouted, and Peter glanced over his shoulder to find Jeremy and Maisie Colton headed out to their car. He tensed and turned away.

Lisa waved back with a bright smile. "Bye, Jeremy."

He'd managed to avoid Maisie for most of the day, until she'd fought her way to the front of the line at the dunking booth. He'd been tempted to leave his post as dunkee before he'd really started his shift, but he'd promised Lisa he'd help. When he'd seen what a bad shot Maisie was, and that his good-natured grin riled her more than jeers, he'd had fun watching the Colton princess make a fool of herself.

Lisa met Peter's gaze and lowered her voice. "I overheard some ladies talking about Maisie earlier."

Peter raised an eyebrow. "Something related to my dad's murder?"

"Perhaps."

Peter closed his tailgate and stepped closer to Lisa. "What did you hear?"

Lisa told him about a conversation between two ladies in the concession line. He'd already known Maisie's reputation for being a loose cannon, but statements the women claimed Maisie had made regarding his father rankled. Maisie's tirade, as repeated by the women, was hearsay and not admissible in court. But it confirmed Peter's suspicion that Maisie held more than a passing grudge against his father. Question was, was Maisie's hostility rooted in family loyalty and her brother's murder conviction, which now appeared to have been a mistake? Or did Maisie have more personal reasons to hate his father? Reasons enough to kill Mark Walsh?

He mulled those questions over as he followed Lisa

back to her house and unloaded the festival miscellany into Lisa's garage.

"Can I offer you something hot to drink as a thank-you?" she asked as they finished moving the last box from his truck.

Peter consulted his watch. Despite the early darkness of the fall evening, it was still early. "Sure."

More than something to drink, he wanted a few minutes with Lisa, without the eyes of the town watching or his son around as a chaperone. He helped Lisa with her coat and hung both his and her coats in the front hall while she started a kettle of water heating.

Peter paused by the rocking chair in the living room long enough to give Samson a ruffle on the head. The cat greeted him with a loud meow, stretched sleepily and half-heartedly bit at his wrist. "Goofy cat," he chuckled as he settled on the sofa, then decided Patrick wasn't off the mark. The fluffy Maine coon had personality to spare. He was no dog, but...

"Here you go." Lisa carried in two mugs of spiced tea and handed one to him as she sat beside him. "Thank you for your help with the festival. I think Patrick had a good time."

"Well, spending time with Patrick wasn't the only reason I went." Setting his mug aside, he scooted closer to Lisa and stroked her cheek with the back of his fingers. "I enjoyed spending the day with you, too."

She smiled sadly then lowered her gaze to her drink. "Peter, I..."

His chest tightened, knowing where her thoughts had drifted. He hated the idea of their relationship hitting a roadblock before it had even started. Turning his hand, he cupped her chin in his palm. "I know you're worried about getting involved with me because of the way your marriage ended. But can't we talk about it?"

She lifted a wistful gaze, her fingers tightening around her mug until her knuckles were bloodless. "Talking doesn't change the facts. I'll never be able to have children, Peter. I can't saddle you or any man with that."

He stroked her bottom lip with his thumb, and her breath hitched. "What if I told you your infertility isn't an issue for me?"

Lisa covered his hand with hers, squeezing his fingers. "I'd say you were either lying to ease my mind, or you hadn't really thought the issue through thoroughly. I've seen how you are with Patrick, heard you talk about your family and how much they mean to you. You can't tell me you don't want more children. I can see the truth in your eyes when you watch your son."

Peter started to deny her assertion but stopped. If he wanted a relationship with Lisa, it had to be based in total honesty. Starting now. He took her drink from her and put it aside, then wrapped his fingers around hers.

"Okay, the truth is I'd like to have more kids one day. Yes. I've always pictured myself with a large family."

With a defeated-sounding sigh, she started to withdraw, and he slid his hand to the base of her skull to keep her from backing out of his reach.

"But more than that, the idea of having more children scares the hell out of me."

Her gaze snapped up to his, dark with concern and confusion. "Scares you?"

"The woman I loved died giving me my son. I know, in here—" he pointed to his head "—that it was a fluke thing. I know the chances that something like that would happen again if I had a baby with another woman are low. But in here—" he splayed a hand over his heart "—I'm terrified of losing someone else I care about. It's been ten years since Katie died, and I still miss her every day. I see her in Patrick, the sacrifice she made to give me my son. That's what you see in my eyes when I look at my boy. Love for him, but also longing for what could have been…if Katie had lived."

Tears glistened in Lisa's eyes. "The children that could have been."

He drew a deep breath. "Partly. But also sadness for all the events Katie is missing. His first steps, first Little League game…school carnivals. Katie would have been a great mom."

With a hiccuping sob, Lisa's face crumpled. "Oh, God." She covered her face with her hands, her shoulders shaking.

Peter's gut pitched. He'd known this conversation would be emotional and difficult, but her breakdown wrenched his gut. "Lisa, honey, what is it?"

She peered up at him with a heartbreaking melancholy etched on her face. "I want all that. I want the first steps, the ball games, the PTA. I want a baby so much it hurts. But I can't. Ever. I had fibroid tumors that necessitated a hysterectomy, so I'll never have my own children—"

"Aw, honey." Peter closed the distance between them and reeled her into his arms, pressing her head to his shoulder. "I'm so sorry. I won't pretend I know how much that must hurt."

"I thought I'd come to terms with it, thought I was doing all right, b-but…" She sniffled and swiped at her damp cheek. "Every day when I go to school and see those young faces in my class, I'm reminded of what I can't have. And I hurt all over again."

She tipped her head back and looked up at him, her expression beseeching him to understand. "That's why

I'm getting my PhD in higher education. I love teaching elementary school, but at the same time it's too painful to continue."

The grief in her voice stabbed him. Peter's chest ached as if sharp talons had raked his flesh and sliced open his heart. He could do nothing to ease her pain, and his sense of helplessness chafed his male ego. Tucking her under his chin again, he squeezed her tighter. "I don't begin to understand why these things happen. It's not fair."

Lisa backed from his embrace and narrowed her wet gaze on his. "I'm not looking for answers why. I know life is unpredictable. You have to take the bad with the good. I've learned to appreciate my blessings—my family in Texas, my health, my home." She stroked his cheek. "Friends who care about me. I just want you to understand why getting involved with you would be a mistake for me."

He dried the moisture on her eyelashes. "Why would it be a mistake?"

She sniffed again and lowered her gaze to her hands. "Being in a relationship would be a lot like teaching elementary school for me. As wonderful as parts of the relationship might be, I'd have a daily reminder of what wasn't possible. Loving a man would make me ache for the children we wouldn't have. There'd always be a gulf between us, something missing. You can't build a future when you start with such a giant hole in the relationship."

Peter held her gaze, his heart pounding wildly. "Then… we have a problem. Because my feelings for you have already grown past simple friendship."

A bittersweet surprise, then regret flittered over her face. "Peter…"

He framed her face with his hands. "I know you feel the same connection between us that I do. The same heat. The same pull." He clenched his teeth and drilled his gaze into hers. "Damn it, Lisa, don't tell me we can't try to make this work. Because I don't think I can stay away."

She sucked in a sharp breath that hissed between her teeth. "But how—"

"I don't know how we'll make it work. I just know we have to try." He nudged her chin up. "I don't want to hurt you, honey. I swear I will do everything in my power to make this work somehow."

Tears sparkled in her eyes. "I'm scared."

He nodded. "I am, too. Putting my heart out there after so many years terrifies me. But I'm in too deep now to do anything else."

She blinked, and fresh tears escaped onto her cheek. Lifting her hand, she raked fingers through his hair before settling her hand on his neck. "Me, too."

Lisa leaned forward and brushed her mouth across his. The brief contact shocked his system like a jolt from a taser. His nerve endings crackled and danced, and his muscles tensed.

Hovering scant inches from him, she angled her gaze to his. "I feel like I'm diving into a murky lake on a hot day," she whispered. Her breaths came quick and light, mingling with his. "I know the water will be cool and refreshing, but I don't know what hidden dangers wait below the surface."

He skimmed her lips with his and murmured, "Go ahead and jump, Lisa. I'll catch you. I'll keep you safe."

"Peter." His name was a sigh as she found his mouth again and kissed him deeply. Desperately. Tenderly.

With one hand cradling her head and his other arm wrapped around her waist, Peter held Lisa close and indulged in the lips he'd been thinking about all day. Heat flashed through him, chasing the chill of past losses from his bones. Lisa's flesh-and-blood kiss was ten times more potent than his daydreams about the stolen kiss by the school office.

Her lips tasted sweet, like spiced tea and warm seduction. She met the pressure of his mouth with her own fervor. When he traced the seam of her lips with his tongue, she opened to him, her contented sigh stoking the fire inside him with promises of future passion.

His body screamed for him to lay her back on the couch and stake his claim to her. But he'd promised not to let her get hurt, and he knew that meant they had to move slowly. His muscles trembled with restraint as he pulled away and finger-combed her hair behind her ear. "I don't want to wait a whole week to see you again."

Smiling, she tipped her head back to meet his gaze. "What do you propose to do about that?"

He grinned, hearing the breathless quality to her voice. Their kiss had left him feeling winded as well. Stunned. Reeling. "Well…my mom and sisters are meeting Patrick and me for dinner tomorrow at Kelley's Cookhouse. Why don't you join us?"

Her eyes widened. "Wow. Meeting the family. Isn't that usually at least a third- or fourth-date kind of thing?"

Her tone was teasing, but he heard an anxious tension behind it as well.

Nudging up her chin with his thumb, he met her dark-eyed gaze. "I don't want to pressure you. I promised we'll take this as slow as you need to."

Lisa caught her bottom lip with her teeth. "I do love barbecue."

He cocked an eyebrow. "Is that a yes?"

She tipped her head and flashed him a lopsided smile. "It is."

"Good." Splaying his fingers, he slid his hand to the

nape of her neck and nudged her forward. "May I kiss you again?"

"Yes, please." She leaned into him, angling her head to seal her mouth with his.

When a tremble shook her, he tightened his hold on her and nuzzled her ear. "We'll figure this out, Lisa. Somehow."

Her fingers dug into his back, and she sighed sadly. "That's the same thing my ex-husband promised…a year before he walked out on our marriage."

Kelley's Cookhouse, owned and operated by the Kelley family for years, was a Honey Creek institution. Everyone who was anyone gathered at the barbecue restaurant at some point during the week to drink a Walsh-brand beer and savor the best smoky ribs and coleslaw west of the Mississippi River. Tonight was no exception. The restaurant, with its dark wood-panel walls and hardwood floors, was packed with Honey Creek residents, family and friends.

Lisa squeezed Peter's hand tighter, so as not to lose him in the crowd, as he led her to a table near the bar where his sisters, Mary and Lucy, were already seated. Mary bore a striking resemblance to Peter's mother, whom Lisa had met yesterday at the festival, but Lucy, with her girl-next-door sweetness and brown eyes, looked more like Peter. Next to Mary, with a possessive arm around her, sat a ruggedly handsome blond-haired man Lisa assumed, based on the coaching Peter had given her on the drive over, was Jake Pierson. The chair beside Lucy was conspicuously empty, a situation Patrick quickly remedied, sliding into the ladder-backed chair and giving his aunt a bear hug.

"Evening, folks," Peter said, as he held out a chair for Lisa. "Everyone, this is Lisa Navarre, Patrick's teacher.

Lisa, this is the motley crew I warned you about in the truck." He gave Lucy a curious glance. "Where's Steve?"

Lisa mentally recalled the list of names Peter had supplied on the drive. Lucy was happily involved with a man named Steve Brown.

"He's caught a nasty cold and didn't feel like coming out tonight." She turned to Patrick and wrapped an arm around the boy's shoulders. "But I didn't want to miss seeing my favorite nephew!"

"I'm your *only* nephew," Patrick groaned.

"But you're still my favorite!"

Lisa turned to Mary, who sat across the table from her. "Peter tells me you and Jake have opened a private security business. How is that going?"

Mary's smile brightened. "So far so good."

As the conversation continued with polite small talk and inquiries about each other's jobs and Lisa's family in Texas, she noticed Peter's gaze roaming the faces in the crowd, his expression speculative, guarded.

"Something wrong?" she whispered to him during a brief lull in the conversation when the waitress arrived to deliver drink orders.

"No, I'm just—" He stopped abruptly, and his expression changed. Shadows of suspicion clouded his face, and his stare grew icy. "I stand corrected. Look who just arrived."

Frowning her concern and curiosity, Lisa pivoted in her chair to glance toward the front door. Darius Colton strode into the main dining room, leading his wife Sharon by the arm. Behind them, Damien, Maisie, Jeremy, Brand and Joan Colton followed, each sweeping the restaurant with gazes ranging from excited, in Jeremy's case, to hostile, in Damien's.

Lisa tensed. "Is this a problem? Can't your family eat

in the same restaurant without it leading to World War Three?"

Peter cut a side glance to his family, presumably checking to see if they'd noticed the new arrivals. "Depends. I don't intend to start anything, but I won't let a slight pass unchecked either."

Lisa sighed. "Peter..."

Darius, the patriarch of the clan, gave the room an imperious glance and, spying the Walshes, glared darkly and spoke to the hostess. He aimed a thumb to the opposite side of the dining room, and the hostess glanced toward the Walsh table and nodded.

The message was clear enough. Darius wanted a table far from the Walshes. Darius took his mousy wife by the arm and led her from the door.

Across the table from Lisa, Lucy's head came up, her gaze darting to the door. She gasped softly, staring at the Colton family. Lisa held her breath, remembering that the youthful infatuation between Damien and Lucy had been a key factor in the families' feud.

"Lucy?" Peter said, leaning toward his sister. "Do you want to leave?"

His sister sent him a sharp look. "Don't be silly. I can't spend the rest of my life ducking and running for cover every time my path crosses his. This is a small town, and we need to figure out how to share it."

"I know, but—" Peter started, but Lucy caught them all off-guard by rising slightly from her chair, smiling and signaling Damien to come to their table.

Peter frowned. "What are you doing?"

Lucy squared her shoulders. "Making peace with my past so I can move forward."

At the front door, Damien nodded, grim-faced, but headed their way. When Maisie grabbed his shirt to stop him, he disengaged his sister's fingers and gave her a push in the opposite direction.

"Damien!" Maisie called after her brother in a panicked voice loud enough to carry through the restaurant.

The din of voices quieted to a murmur as heads swivelled to follow the unfolding drama.

Lisa reached for Peter, who looked ready to jump Damien with the slightest provocation, and wrapped her hand around his wrist. When he met her eyes, she sent him a quelling look.

Damien's boots scuffed the hardwood floor as he stepped up to their table and cast a dark look to the Walshes.

Chapter 11

Despite Lucy's warning look, Peter rose to his feet and raised his chin, as if putting Damien on notice. Lisa held her breath, much as she sensed everyone else gathered in the restaurant did.

But when Damien's gaze landed on Lucy, a flicker of warmth lit his eyes, though his mouth stayed pressed in a firm line. "Lucy."

Lucy flashed a nervous smile. "Hello, Damien. It's nice to see you."

Damien's brow furrowed, and he grunted. "Right."

Lucy squared her shoulders, her smile dimming. "It is. I...I never wanted you to suffer because of—"

"Whatever." His tone was cool, flat. "You wanted something?"

Mary, Jake and Peter exchanged worried looks. Lisa could have cut the tension with a knife. Even Patrick seemed to notice the hostile undercurrent. Sidling closer to Lucy, Patrick eyed the tall, dark-haired stranger looming over their table.

"Just…to say hello." She cleared her throat, and her fingers trembled as she fidgeted with her silverware. "And I'm sorry about…everything that happened. I—"

"Sorry? You never wrote, never came to see me. Not once," Damien interrupted. Lisa swore she heard pain laced heavily throughout his hard tone, and her heart broke for the star-crossed high-school sweethearts Damien and Lucy had been.

Lucy dropped her gaze for the first time and drew a deep breath. "I'm sorry for that, too. I was as hurt and confused about everything as you were, and—"

Damien scoffed. "You think so? I was in prison, Lu. Accused of a murder I didn't commit. Abandoned by you, by members of my family. You really think you were hurting as much as I was?"

Lisa wondered if anyone else noticed Damien's use of a nickname for Lucy. That he still thought of her in terms of the intimate pet name spoke volumes to Lisa.

Peter took a step toward Damien. "Look, Colton, if you think—"

"Peter." Lucy's firm tone stopped her brother. Shoving her chair back, she circled the end of the table to where Damien stood. When she lightly touched Damien's arm, he jerked, as if jolted by lightning.

Lisa's fingers clutched the arm of her chair. She recognized the raw emotion that filled Damien's face. Bitterness clashed with longing, betrayed love, remorse and regret battled anger and disappointment. When Ray had walked out on their marriage, she'd felt many of the same conflicting feelings that marched across Damien's face. His jaw tightened, evidence that he was working hard to maintain a stony facade and shove down the rioting feelings.

"I know we can't change the past," Lucy said softly. "But I don't want to be enemies going forward. I won't ask you to pretend we're friends again, but can we at least be civil when we meet in town?"

Damien shifted his feet slightly, and the hard line of his jaw relaxed a degree. "That shouldn't be a problem, seeing as how I'm leaving town."

Lucy frowned. "Leaving?"

"This town holds too many ghosts. I'm planning on heading down to Nevada. Maybe starting my own ranch." He paused and sighed wearily. "I need a fresh start. That's not possible here in Honey Creek."

"Oh…" Lucy fumbled. "Well, good luck. I…" She hesitated as if torn what to do next, what to say. Then, taking a deep breath, she grabbed Damien's hand, rose on her toes and kissed his cheek.

A murmur rolled through the restaurant, and Lisa sensed more than saw Peter stiffen.

"Take care of yourself, Damien," Lucy said quietly before sinking back on her heels again. When she would have withdrawn her hand, Damien squeezed Lucy's fingers, drawing her gaze back to his. For several seconds he said nothing, his green eyes boring down on Lucy with an intensity that sent a shiver through Lisa.

"Goodbye, Lu," he said at last, while still clinging to her hand. His throat worked as he swallowed, before he added a rasped, "and thanks" as he turned quickly and strode away.

Lucy watched him leave, her expression poignant and filled with wistful regret.

Lisa's heart thudded, touched by the bittersweet goodbye between the former lovers.

The gazes of the other diners followed Damien's retreat, dividing speculative stares between Lucy and the brooding ex-con Colton. Lisa wanted to shout at the room to mind their own business. She couldn't imagine being a member of one of the town's prominent families and having so much attention drawn to her every move. Yet if she started dating Peter, wouldn't that put her in the gossip limelight? She wasn't sure how she felt about that.

Peter stepped closer to his sister and touched her arm. "You okay?"

Lucy rallied, flashing Peter a bright smile. "I'm fine. Hey, I've got Steve now. And my store, my family. I'm great!" She clapped her hands together as she spun back to the table. "So what are we ordering? I'm starved!"

Peter continued to watch his sister with his brow knitted, so Lisa leaned over to him and put a supportive hand on his arm. "She's not the vulnerable teenager she was back then, Peter. She's okay. And I think they both needed that closure."

He shifted his worried look to Lisa. "Maybe, but he—"

"No maybes. Look at her." Lisa nodded her head toward Lucy, who was laughing with Mary over something Patrick said. "She's doing all right. She's putting the past behind her. So is Mary. Please, Peter, they have a right to move on and be happy with where their lives are taking them now."

Peter drew a slow sigh and nodded. "You're right. But seeing him here after all these years just…shook something loose deep inside. I didn't do enough to protect her fifteen years ago, and I don't intend to make the same mistake again."

Peter's obvious love and protectiveness for his sister touched a tender spot in Lisa's heart. If she gave in to the call of her heart, if she let herself fall for Peter, would he be that supportive of her? She'd been on her own, away from her family in Texas so long, the idea of someone looking out for her, having her back through the tough times in life held tremendous appeal. Carrying the load alone grew wearisome at times. She missed having someone close to lean on in difficult times. And the months since her divorce had been *very* difficult.

Knowing how much Peter cared about his family and looked out for their best interests spoke volumes regarding his character and priorities. Had she really accused him of having his priorities mixed up the day she called him to the school about Patrick's misbehavior?

She saw now that Peter was, in fact, a single father, juggling his son's needs with his career and a cascade of recent family tragedies. That was a lot for anyone, and if Peter was overwhelmed by it all, that only made him human, not irresponsible.

Lucy caught Lisa's eye, pulling her out of her thoughts briefly. "Save room for dessert. The chocolate cake here is the best! Right, Patrick?"

"Oh, yeah!" Patrick gushed.

She smiled at them. "Oh, I'm well acquainted with the chocolate cake here. In fact, maybe I'll skip dinner and go straight to dessert."

Peter arched an eyebrow. "Can't recommend that. You don't want to miss the barbecued ribs."

Jolene Walsh arrived at last, took a seat next to Peter, and pulled off a pair of leather driving gloves. "Sorry I'm late. The doctor came in right as I was leaving Craig at the hospital. He said Craig's making good progress and can likely go home on Monday." Her smile lit her face, pure relief radiating from her every pore. "Craig sends his love to everyone, by the way." She sent a glowing look around the table to her children and grandson. "So what did I miss?"

"Oh, nothing much," Lucy chirped. "We were just discussing what to order." Without any further mention of Damien or the Coltons, Lucy waved to their waitress.

Once their order had been taken, conversation turned to yesterday's Fall Festival at the school, and the upcoming Thanksgiving holiday.

"I want everyone to plan on coming to the ranch for our family dinner next Thursday," Jolene announced, then turned to Lisa. "You're welcome to come with Peter, dear. We'd love to have you join us."

Lisa blinked, startled—and flattered—by the invitation. "Oh, well, thank you. I—"

Peter and Patrick both sent her expectant, eager looks.

"Can you, Ms. Navarre? Please?" Patrick asked.

Her gaze shifted to Peter, who lifted a dark eyebrow in query. "No pressure. If it's too much too fast…"

"I'd love to join you," Lisa said, facing Jolene. "What can I bring?"

"I have a new recipe for a low-sugar, low-fat pie I want to bring," Mary interjected.

As the conversation continued, planning the menu for Thanksgiving dinner, Lucy pushed her chair back and rose. "If you'll excuse me for a minute, I'm going to make a quick trip to the ladies' room."

Mary pushed her chair back, too. "Want some company?"

"Sure. Lisa?" Lucy hitched her head, inviting Lisa to follow her.

Mary gave Jake a teasing stern look. "No comments from the peanut gallery about women traveling in packs to the restroom."

Jake turned up a palm. "What? Did I say anything?"

Mary gave her fiancé a quick kiss and a smile as she stepped away from the table, then hooked her arm in Lisa's as they fell in step behind Lucy. "I have to tell you, I haven't seen my brother smiling as much in years as he has been these last couple weeks. I'd bet money you are the reason."

Lisa felt heat sting her cheeks. "I, uh—"

Lucy came to an abrupt stop in front of them, and Mary and Lisa ran into her.

"You!" Maisie Colton blocked their entry to the women's restroom, hands on her hips, glaring at Lucy with a venomous snarl. "You have a lot of nerve hitting on my brother like that after what you and your family did to him!"

Lucy fell back a step, clearly startled by the attack. Mary moved up next to Lucy, and Lisa flanked Peter's sister from the other side, her heart thumping anxiously. Maisie's infamous volatility worried Lisa. She didn't want the families to engage in a public brawl.

Lucy raised her chin, and calmly replied, "I didn't hit on Damien, Maisie. Not that it is any of your business."

Maisie puffed out her chest and narrowed her eyes. "My brother will always be my business. And I'm warning you to stay away from him! Haven't you hurt him enough?"

"Come on, Luce." Mary nudged her sister's arm. "Ignore her."

But Lucy squared her shoulders and faced Maisie's challenging glare. "I have no intention of hurting your brother. For your information, I'm happily engaged and moving on with my life."

Maisie gave a disgruntled sniff. "Yeah, I heard you were engaged. Poor guy doesn't know what he's getting himself into." Her gaze suddenly shifted to Lisa's. "Be warned, Ms. Navarre. The Walshes are cold-hearted and self-serving. If you were smart, you'd run the other way. Peter may seem like a catch, but he will break your heart. It's just what the Walshes do."

Lisa was so stunned by Maisie's unwanted advice, she didn't notice Damien's approach until he loomed over the women with a dark expression. He wrapped a firm hand around his sister's arm and tugged her away from her confrontational stance in front of Lucy. "Go back to the table, Maisie. You're out of line."

Maisie sent her brother a hurt look. "I'm just defending you. You can't let the Walshes push you around!"

"No one is pushing me around. Don't hassle Lucy ever again. Understand?" Damien's tone brooked no resistance.

Maisie stared at her brother as if he'd lost his mind. "Do you not remember what they did to us? The Walshes—"

"Maisie." The deep resonant voice of Darius Colton interrupted Maisie's tirade.

Lisa lifted her gaze to the senior Colton who now stood behind Damien. A muscle in Darius's jaw jumped, and he narrowed a warning stare on his daughter. "Don't make a scene and embarrass the family."

Maisie frowned. "But, Daddy—"

"You heard me." His tone was final.

With an indignant huff, Maisie lifted her nose and stormed back to the Colton's table. Darius said nothing else before turning and walking away, but Damien divided an uneasy look between Mary, Lucy and Lisa. "I'm sorry about that, ladies."

"Forget it. Come on, Lucy." Mary gave Damien a tight, stiffly cordial nod, then wrapped her arm in her sister's and steered Lucy toward the restroom.

Lisa knew she should follow the Walsh sisters, but the look on Damien's face gave her pause. The man, for all his gruff posturing, was clearly hurting. He'd had a less-than-warm welcome home from his family, if the rumor mill was correct, and after witnessing the scene between him and Lucy earlier, Lisa felt compelled to say something to him. But what?

Damien Colton's problems and heartaches weren't any of her business. But being no stranger to pain and rejection herself, Lisa felt an empathetic tug for him.

"I—" she started then stalled when his jade gaze met hers.

"You're Lisa Navarre, aren't you?"

She gaped at Damien, stunned that he knew her name. "Uh, yes."

"You teach at the elementary school, right?"

Lisa laughed nervously. "How did you—?"

Damien's cheek twitched in a quick grin. "My nephew said something earlier when he saw you at the Walshes' table. You were, apparently, his favorite teacher."

Lisa's cheeks heated, and she smiled. "I think pretty highly of Jeremy, too. He's a bright boy and well-mannered."

Damien's expression warmed with obvious affection for his nephew. "Thank you."

Lisa shifted her feet awkwardly, fully aware of Peter's hawk-eyed gaze watching her exchange with the ex-con.

Sticking his hands in his back pockets, Damien angled his head and gave Lisa a speculative look. "I know what Peter's probably telling you about my family."

Lisa's heart thudded. She didn't want to be drawn into this conversation…

"I know there is no love lost between your families."

"Yeah. You could say that. But…" He paused, glancing away, as if looking for the right words. As he brought his gaze back to her, Damien did a double take. His attention snagged on someone at the front door, and though he tried to cover his distraction, Lisa didn't miss the obvious signs of male interest in the lift of his brow and widening of his pupils. She turned to see who had caught Damien's eye.

Eve Kelley, looking especially radiant with her hair upswept and wearing a high-waisted blue dress that complemented her coloring, stood by the hostess desk waiting to be seated.

Lisa hid the grin that tugged her lips. "That's Eve Kelley. She owns Salon Allegra. Would you like me to introduce you?"

"Huh. Oh, no, I—" Damien rolled his muscled shoulders and furrowed his brow, as if embarrassed to have been caught ogling the blond beauty. "I remember her. She was in Perry's class. Cheerleader. Beauty queen. Miss Popular." He shook his head. "Not my type." He clenched his back teeth, his jaw tensing. "Anyway, just remember there are two sides to every story. Anything Peter tells you about my family is only half the picture."

That Damien would defend his family to her, be concerned about her perception of the Coltons—especially in light of what she'd heard through the grapevine about the family's strained relationship with Damien when he went to prison—only bolstered her instincts about the brooding man. Despite the gruff persona he projected, she sensed the wounded soul behind the dark scowl and shadowed eyes. And her heart went out to him.

She held his gaze and nodded. "I'll keep that in mind. Good night, Damien. It was nice to meet you."

He jerked a nod, then headed back to his table just as Lucy and Mary emerged from the restroom.

Mary gave her a concerned look. "More trouble?"

"No, we were…talking about his nephew. I taught Jeremy and…" Lisa shrugged and let her sentence trail off.

"We'll wait for you if you still need the facilities."

Lucy hitched her thumb over her shoulder toward the bathroom door.

"Naw. I'm good, and—" she glanced back at their table "—it looks like our dinner has arrived."

Peter stood as she approached and pulled out her chair. "Should I be jealous of your heart-to-heart with Damien?"

She smiled brightly and kissed his cheek. "Not at all."

Though she could tell he wanted more explanation of what she'd discussed with the ex-con, she said nothing else.

The rest of their dinner passed uneventfully. Despite the drama that had started the evening, the Walshes shared a sumptuous meal, laughed over stories they told on each other, and made plans for a family Thanksgiving. Being included in the family's camaraderie filled an empty place in Lisa's heart that had been languishing in the years since her divorce. But her inclusion in the Walsh family plans was bittersweet. As much as she craved the connections of a large family, the evening only demonstrated to her how much Peter loved his family, needed his family, deserved to have the family she couldn't give him.

Last night, she'd promised Peter she'd give their relationship a chance. Yet the closer she got to Peter and his family, the clearer it became to her that she was headed to another heartache. She simply couldn't give Peter the kind of relationship he deserved.

Chapter 12

Monday morning, Peter finished up a case report earlier than he'd expected and found himself downtown with time on his hands before he was due to meet with a new client. He sat in his truck, drumming his fingers on his steering wheel and considering the best use of his time.

He wished he could surprise Patrick by stopping by the school for lunch but the class didn't break for lunch for another hour.

Peter smiled, remembering the family dinner at Kelley's Cookhouse the night before. Lisa had fitted right in with his sisters and mother. And they seemed to like her, going so far as to make plans for shopping on Black Friday together. He'd gotten a chance to get to know Jake Pierson better and knew the former FBI agent was a good match for his sister. Jake would keep Mary safe.

The evening had been nearly perfect. Nearly. Peter gritted his teeth, remembering Damien Colton's glowering indignation and Maisie's repeat performance, confronting Mary, Lucy and Lisa. The Coltons were like a bad rash, a constant source of irritation. Some days, Peter just wanted to meet the Colton clan in the center of town and have an old-fashioned duel. The town just didn't seem big enough for both families. Something had to give.

Peter cranked his engine, which sputtered to life, protesting the Montana cold. Without conscious decision, he headed for the sheriff's office. Two weeks had passed since he'd last confronted Wes Colton, and he hadn't seen any hint of progress in the investigation in that time. Nothing in the *Honey Creek Gazette*. No calls from the sheriff's office. Zilch.

Acid churned in Peter's gut as he parked in front of the redbrick building that housed the sheriff's office. He recognized Wes Colton's vehicle in the lot, telling him the sheriff should be in his office.

He strode inside and approached the receptionist's desk. "I want to see the sheriff."

The female officer looked up, clearly recognized him and hesitated before paging her boss's office. "Sheriff Colton, Peter Walsh is here to see you."

Wes didn't reply for several seconds. Finally a mumbled curse word filtered through the intercom, followed by a grudging, "Send him back."

The sheriff was on his feet behind his desk when Peter entered his office.

"Morning, Peter. What can I do for you?" he said with strained civility.

Peter braced his feet and squared his shoulders. "I still haven't heard anything from you about the investigations into my father's murder or Craig Warner's poisoning. I can only assume that means nothing's being done, no progress is being made."

Wes gave him a patronizing grin. "You'd be wrong. I'm not required to report my findings to you or anyone until my case is wrapped up. So don't assume my silence indicates anything other than the facts of the case are a police matter and not for public consumption."

"I'm family of the victim." Peter jabbed Wes's desk with a finger.

"Which makes you a possible suspect."

Peter gaped at the sheriff. "You've got to be kidding. My alibi was confirmed months ago."

Wes shrugged. "I'm still not discussing the case with you."

"I have a right to know what's happening!"

"I disagree."

Peter clenched his back teeth and swallowed the retort on his lips. Clearly getting into the same argument with Wes wouldn't get him anywhere. He thought a moment and decided on a surprise attack.

"Who fathered Maisie's son?"

Wes blinked. Frowned. "Excuse me?"

"Who is Jeremy's father? There is no name listed on his birth certificate."

Wes tensed and drew himself taller. "How did you get a copy of Jeremy's birth certificate?"

"I'm a private investigator. I have resources, tricks to get around red tape."

"If you've done something illegal—"

"You'll never prove it." Peter braced his hands on the sheriff's desk and leaned toward him. "Answer my question. Who is Jeremy's father?"

Wes hesitated. "Maisie would never say."

"Why did she leave town so abruptly back in 1995, right after my dad disappeared?"

Wes scowled and folded his arms over his chest. "I think you know the answer to that."

"The obvious answer is because she was hiding her pregnancy to avoid scandal. But when she returned with a son in tow, she kinda blew that cover, didn't she?"

The sheriff sighed wearily. "What's your point Walsh?"

"I think your sister had an affair with my father that went sour." Peter smiled his satisfaction when the color drained from Wes's face. "I think Jeremy is Mark Walsh's son, and that your sister killed him to keep her secret a secret. Or out of revenge for his dumping her."

Wes twisted his mouth in a dismissive frown. "That's insane. My sister is brash and confrontational, but she's not a killer."

"You sure about that? She's been rather vocal around town, saying how glad she is that my dad is gone and that he got what he deserved."

The sheriff lifted a hand in concession. "Not particularly discreet of her, I admit. But I know my sister. She's not a killer."

"Does she have an alibi for the time of my father's death?"

Wes dragged a hand down his cheek. "I'm doing my job, Walsh. I don't need you to back-seat drive."

Peter aimed a finger at Wes. "You do if you are driving with blinders on concerning your family. They should be at the top of your suspect list."

Wes drew in a deep breath and blew it out, his jaw tense. "So you've said. Your five minutes with me are up. Goodbye, Peter."

The sheriff sat down behind his desk, flipped open a file and bent over it, signaling an end to the discussion.

Peter didn't budge. "At least tell me what direction you're

going with the case. Who are you investigating? What are your leads? God, give me something!"

Wes leaned back in his chair, tapping his pen on his desk in visible irritation. "Walsh, this case is bigger than just a murder investigation or a case of intentional poisoning. There are people working this case from more angles than you could imagine. But because of the sensitive nature of the ongoing investigation, and because I don't want to jeopardize the case, I can't tell you anything more. I told you once and I'll tell you again. Butt out." Wes leaned forward, stabbing the air with his pen to punctuate his demand. "If you interfere with the investigation or compromise the case in any way, I'll write you up for obstructing justice."

"If so many people are on this case, why is it taking so long to close it? Three members of my family have been attacked in five months. I refuse to sit by while your officers chase their tails and let my family get hurt again. I want answers, Wes. I deserve answers. And my family deserves justice. If you can't get it for us, then by God, I will."

Wes narrowed his eyes and lowered his voice. "Don't do anything rash, Peter. You'll have your justice soon enough. We just need a little more time."

Jamming his hands in his coat pockets, Peter met Wes's stare. "You've had five months. Time is up." With that, he turned and stalked from the sheriff's office.

In the parking lot, he slammed his truck door and sat for a moment brooding.

…this case is bigger than just a murder investigation or a case of intentional poisoning. There are people working this case from more angles than you could imagine.

What did Wes mean by that? How big was the investigation? He gritted his teeth as he backed out of his parking space. He hated being kept in the dark. Wes knew something, and it irritated the hell out of Peter that Wes wouldn't tell him. For that matter, Mary and Jake had been awfully cagey when he questioned them a couple weeks ago. They knew something they weren't sharing as well. And his mom—what did she know about his dad that she was keeping secret?

He slammed his hand on the steering wheel in frustration. He loved his family, but they had more secrets than the CIA. They might think they were protecting him by keeping him in the dark, but information was power. How was he supposed to protect his family if he didn't know what he was up against?

That Tuesday, Peter and Jolene met Patrick at his school for the class Thanksgiving feast. As he sat at the long lunchroom table eating his cafeteria-prepared turkey and stuffing, Peter watched Lisa greet the other parents and mill about the crowd, wishing students a happy holiday.

When she finally made it to their table, she slid into a seat and blew out a tired breath. "Whew! I'm ready for our holiday break. How about you, Patrick?"

He nodded. "I ain't gonna do nothing all day tomorrow but watch TV and play video games."

She arched an eyebrow and laugh-sighed. "Good to know my grammar lessons have made a difference for you, Patrick."

Peter ruffled his son's hair. "Sounds to me like you need to crack a school book instead of cranking up the games, sport."

His son's eyes rounded. "What? Not on vacation, Dad."

Jolene nudged her son with her shoulder. "So what are your plans tomorrow? Will you need Grandma to ride herd on the little anti-grammarian?"

Peter caught Lisa's gaze. "Are we still on for the sleigh ride and picnic at the ranch?"

"You really want to picnic in this weather?" She aimed her thumb toward the cafeteria window. Outside, a light snow fell and blanketed the ground.

He reached for her hand. "I promise to make a bonfire and have plenty of blankets and hot coffee."

She turned her palm over and gave his fingers a squeeze before withdrawing her hand. "Then I accept."

He smiled and cast a side glance to his mother. "Then I'll need your services with the anti-grammarian."

Patrick took in the adults with an encompassing glance and shook his head. "Parents are so lame."

Peter chuckled and had a bite of turkey halfway to his mouth when Patrick said, "Ms. Navarre, when we're not at school, is it okay if I call you Mom?"

The question kicked Peter in the gut, and he lowered his fork to his plate with a clatter.

Lisa choked on the fruit juice she sipped. Her panicked eyes darted to Peter's, and she had to cough a few times before she could speak. "Uh, well, Patrick, isn't that a little premature? Your dad and I aren't married."

"Yet. But you're dating now, right? Isn't it just a matter of time?"

"Patrick." Peter sent Lisa an apologetic look. "It's rather rude to put Ms. Navarre on the spot like this. If and when she's ready to have you call her anything besides Ms. Navarre, she'll tell you. Until then, it's Ms. Navarre. Capisce?"

Patrick's shoulders drooped. "Yes, sir."

Peter's heart performed a slow roll in his chest. Was Patrick's eagerness to call Lisa Mom an indication of his son's longing for a mother or of his growing attachment to his teacher as a mother figure? Or both? When he'd asked

Lisa to give their relationship a chance, Peter hadn't fully thought out the ramifications where Patrick was concerned. And what kind of father did that make him? Why hadn't he realized that his involvement with Lisa meant his son would be forming delicate bonds to her as well? Patrick stood to get hurt if things didn't work out with Lisa.

An uneasy apprehension crawled through Peter. Tomorrow, he and Lisa needed to reach an understanding. He couldn't let her fears regarding their budding relationship come back to haunt Patrick. The tragedies of the past months with his grandfather's murder, the attack on his aunt, and Craig Warner's poisoning had already shaken Patrick's world. Losing a mother figure would be too much. Peter had to make sure that didn't happen.

The day before Thanksgiving dawned sunny and cold. The fresh layer of snow made perfect conditions for the horse-drawn sleigh.

"The family bought the sleigh from an antiques dealer about ten years ago for days just like today," Peter told her as he hitched the ranch's strongest horse to the sleigh and helped Lisa climb onto the seat.

She pulled one of the lap blankets around her legs as she settled in. "Peter, this is pure Currier and Ives! I can't think of a better way to start my Thanksgiving holiday."

"Glad you think so," he replied, his breath forming a white cloud between them when he spoke. "Patrick was chomping at the bit to come with us. I had to promise him he could ride our stallion, Lightning, on the property when we come for dinner tomorrow as consolation."

"You should have let him come. He'd have had fun today."

He sent her a side glance as he gathered the reigns. "Maybe so. But today is about us."

His emphasis on the word *us* stirred a flutter in her chest. Peter had arranged a romantic setting, a sumptuous picnic and complete privacy. He'd carefully planned a perfect day. So why was she so apprehensive about where their picnic would lead?

Despite her promise to give her relationship with Peter a chance, she was scared of serious involvement, terrified of repeating the cycle of pain that had broken up her marriage. Even the thought of it left a pit in her stomach and a cold sweat on her lip. She couldn't go to that dark place in her life again.

Regret settled in her chest, colder than the ice and snow crusted over the sprawling fields. She hated being of two minds regarding Peter—wanting him and his son in her life, yet fearing what seemed inevitable: more heartache and devastation.

With a flick of the reigns, Peter sent the horse clopping over the snow-covered fields of the Walsh family ranch. Tiny bells on the horse's harness jingled, reminding Lisa of numerous Christmas carols. She snuggled closer to Peter as the sleigh whisked over the open land toward the woods on the far side of the property. She could already see a large stack of firewood he'd set up for their bonfire.

When they pulled to a stop, Peter jumped to the ground, then turned to lift Lisa down from the sleigh. Even through thick layers of clothing, the contact made her skin tingle. Or maybe it was the look of pure seduction in Peter's gaze as he let her body slide along his as he lowered her feet to the ground. Before he released her, he caught her mouth for a body-warming kiss that promised much more to come. Lisa's heart pattered with anticipation.

Peter lifted down a large basket and a tarpaulin from the back of the sled. "I had the Honey-B Café fix our lunch. I hope you're hungry."

Yes, but for you. Not food. Lisa squelched the thought and took one end of the tarp to help him spread the ground cover next to the pile of firewood.

"Cold weather always gives me a good appetite."

Peter grinned. "Good. If you'll get that blanket and lay it out on top of the tarp, I'll light the fire."

"You've already lit my fire." Lisa shook out the quilt Peter indicated, and as she smoothed the wrinkles, she glanced up to find Peter looking at her with a devilish smile tugging his mouth. She hesitated a beat, then gasped. "Did I say that out loud?"

Peter threw back his head and laughed. "Funny how I was thinking the same thing."

He tossed a match on the firewood, which instantly roared to life. Clearly he'd soaked the wood with lighter fluid earlier. Peter dropped onto the blanket beside her, pulling her into his arms. "Do you know what I'm most thankful for this Thanksgiving?"

The answer shone from his eyes, and Lisa's chest filled with a happiness she hadn't known in years. She wanted to bottle the feeling and save it for days to come when she knew the loneliness and disappointment would creep back into her life.

With a teasing grin, she smoothed her cold hands over his warm, bristly cheeks. "I'll take a guess and say delivery pizza."

He cocked his head as if considering her answer. "Hmm, good point. But no." His dark eyes honed in on hers, his gaze hot and enticing. "You, Lisa. I'm so thankful that I met you."

A bittersweet ache throbbed in her chest. She wanted to believe meeting Peter was meant to be, that maybe her luck had turned for the best. But doubt demons bit hard, spoiling the tender moment. *It can't last. You can only give him heartbreak and grief.*

Ducking her chin, she battled the surge of melancholy. "Peter, I can't—"

"Don't." His finger touched her lips, and her pulse scampered. His gaze drilled hers with a steely conviction. "You promised to give me a chance. No second-guessing, no regrets. Let me in, Lisa. Let me be the man who gives you back your hopes and dreams."

In that moment, she knew she'd lost another little piece of her heart to Peter. His determination to be with her, despite the costs she'd laid out, burrowed into the cracks Ray had left in her soul.

She leaned in to him and brushed her lips on his. "I'm thankful for you, too, Peter."

Peter deepened the kiss, locking her in a firm embrace and sandwiching her body between his hard chest and the unyielding ground. In his arms, Lisa savored a sense of security and protection she'd missed in recent years. Yet at the same time, she felt as if she were spinning along a race track, out of control, headed for a crash. The dichotomy wrestled uneasily inside her.

When Peter broke the kiss and sat up, she sucked in unsteady breaths, trying to regain her balance, yet cherishing the dizzying rush of sweet sensation he stirred in her.

He pulled a bottle of champagne and two flutes from the basket. The cork exited with the appropriate *pop,* and after pouring two glasses, Peter shoved the bottle down in the snow and handed her a flute. "To new beginnings and seeing where this path leads."

He touched his glass to hers and drank deeply, his bedroom eyes holding hers. Even before she sipped the bubbly wine, warmth and longing flowed through her. The champagne tickled her tongue and, on her empty stomach, soon had her head feeling muzzy.

"I think we should crack open that basket of goodies, or I'm going to be tipsy in a minute."

Peter wiggled his eyebrows. "Ah, my evil plan is working…"

Chuckling, she curled her fingers into his suede coat and snuggled closer. "Evil but genius. Kiss me again, you dastardly man."

He did, and soon lunch was forgotten.

Beside the crackling fire, with a crisp blue winter sky above, Lisa lost herself in Peter's kisses, the tenderness of his touch and the seductive rumble of pleasure that vibrated in his chest. When they finally did open the lunch basket, they lingered for hours, feeding each other cheese and crackers, grapes and sinfully rich cream puffs. They nibbled sandwiches and savored an artichoke dip and tortilla chips.

And through it all, they shared intimate chit-chat about their hopes and dreams, their hurts and heartaches, while restless hands roamed and tantalized. The exchanged slow, sultry kisses that intoxicated her more than the champagne ever could.

As their passion grew, Peter slid his hands under Lisa's coat and sweater, his touch shockingly cold against her warm skin. She gasped at the contact, as a shiver chased through her, then moaned her delight when his hand cupped her breast and grazed her nipple. In turn, she unbuttoned the flannel shirt he wore and raked her fingers down his bared chest, memorizing the feel of his taut skin and muscle under her hands. When he shivered, she couldn't be sure whether it was from the cold or her touch.

Nuzzling his ear, she whispered, "As lovely as this picnic

is, I'm not sure this is the weather or the best location for what I think is on both our minds."

Beneath her hands, a shudder rippled through Peter. "Let me douse the fire, and we'll head back to the ranch. Since my mom is with Patrick, we'll have the place to ourselves."

Anticipation ramped through Lisa, leaving her body jangling and flushed. "Perfect."

When Peter returned from settling the horse in its stable, Lisa was waiting beside the fire she'd lit in the living-room grate.

"Can I get you anything from the kitchen?" he offered, still playing the perfect host.

She twisted her mouth in a come-hither smile and tugged her sweater off over her head. "What I want isn't in the kitchen."

Peter cocked an eyebrow and returned a simmering grin. "Do tell."

Instead she showed him.

His gaze heated as she lowered the zipper on her jeans and stepped out of them. Crossing to him, she slid her hands over his broad chest, then looped her arms around his neck. "Where were we?"

His palms skimmed down her back and cupped her bottom. Sinking his fingers into her, he pulled her flush with his body. "This seems like a good place to start."

Angling his head, he sealed his mouth over hers and swept his tongue in to duel with hers. With greedy hands, she untucked his shirt and pulled it, still buttoned, over his head. Tossing the shirt aside, she canted back to fumble with the zipper at his fly. In seconds, he'd helped her strip off his jeans, and they stood flesh to flesh, warming the chill from their bones with deep lingering kisses and the eager exploration of their hands.

Dragging a quilt from the couch, Peter made them a hasty makeshift bed on the floor in front of the fireplace. She knelt beside him on the quilt and sank into his open arms, shutting out the nagging doubts about their future. Right now, all she wanted was Peter. She wanted to be a sensual, sexual woman and not the barren vessel she'd felt like at the end of her relationship with Ray. She wanted carnal, satisfying sex, not the mechanical, result-oriented process that had dominated most of her marriage. She wanted to feel desirable. Alive.

And in return, she held nothing back. Lisa tuned out her inhibitions and let herself indulge in the passion Peter awoke in her.

Their legs tangled, their mouths fused, their hands explored.

While Peter nibbled the curve of her throat, she curled her fingers into his back and writhed sensuously against him. A pounding heat built in her core, crackling in her blood like the fire in the grate. She savored the sensation of his skin against hers, the way his chest hair teased her nipples. Peter moved his kisses down her collarbone and into the valley between her breasts, while his hands traced the curve of her hip and trailed lightly along her thigh, his fingers stirring tendrils of desire in their wake. When he levered himself up to gaze tenderly into her eyes, her heart performed a forward roll. Without her protective shields in place, she could fall hard and fast for this loving man.

"You're beautiful," he murmured, his expression echoing his words.

And you're the answer to a prayer. She closed her eyes, when the sting of unwanted tears gathered in her sinuses. *Don't think. Just feel. Savor.*

Dipping his head, he drew her peaked breast into his mouth and she arched her back, offering herself to him. Ribbons of tingling heat shot through her as his tongue lashed and aroused. She sighed her pleasure and worked her hands between them to stroke the hard shaft that he pressed against her thigh.

He drew a sharp breath as her fingers skimmed the heat and length of him. "Lisa…"

"Now," she whispered, opening herself to him.

With a throaty groan, he sank into her, filling her—fulfilling her.

Their bodies swayed and rocked in the rhythm as old as time, and as the coil of need tightened in her core, Lisa felt a connection to Peter that went beyond the joining of bodies. Something elemental, spiritual, intimate.

And frightening.

She was falling in love with Peter Walsh.

Peter shuddered as he climaxed, the release so powerful it shook him to his marrow. His whole body throbbed and every nerve ending sparked. It had been a long time since he'd been with a woman, but he couldn't blame his recent celibacy for the surge of emotions that battered him in the wake of the hottest, sweetest lovemaking he'd known in years.

Peter wrapped his arms around Lisa, holding her close to the heavy thud of his heart. Pure joy and a sense of completeness swelled in his chest until he thought he might burst with it. He remembered feeling like this when he'd married Katie. He'd known then, as he did now, that he'd found someone he would love the rest of his life.

Love. He smiled as the word tickled his mind, and he kissed the top of her head.

Lisa drew lazy circles on his chest with her finger, and

his body answered with a fresh surge of heat and desire. He wanted her again.

He wanted her forever.

He'd sidestepped and ignored the truth for days, trying to give Lisa the time and space she needed to be comfortable with their growing closeness. But after making love to her, sharing the ultimate union of body and soul with her, he couldn't deny his feelings any longer.

"Lisa," he murmured, his lips pressed softly to her temple.

She tipped her head back and met his gaze through a drowsy screen of eyelashes.

"I know what we talked about the other night…about how we should take things slow, give you a chance to get comfortable with our relationship, but this—"

He stroked a hand down her back and felt her tremble as she hummed her pleasure. "No regrets, Peter. We both wanted this. Despite our haste, I knew what I was doing."

He thought about their eager battle to shed their clothes, and a chuckle rumbled from his chest. "Yes, you did. And you did it well."

She flashed an impish grin, and he couldn't resist kissing the sassy smile. Fire licked his veins, his hunger for her returning in force. The magic of her lips was almost enough to make him lose his line of thought. But four words pounded in his brain, demanding to be shared.

After raking her hair back from her face, he held her head between his hands and stared deeply into her warm eyes. "I love you, Lisa."

Lisa gasped softly, and her brow twitched in a frown. Though she grew still outside, frozen by shock, her insides were a farrago of emotions. For a moment, she wondered if she'd misunderstood Peter. But with a glow in his gaze, he repeated the words that sent a frisson of fear to her marrow.

"I haven't felt like this for anyone since Katie died, and I can't pretend this is just a casual thing for me. I want you in my life, Lisa. Always."

She struggled for a breath, pushing against his chest to free herself from his grasp. He'd promised not to rush her, to give her time. She'd made love to him because she was powerfully attracted to him, and the moment had felt right. Yet suddenly their relationship was careening down a path she hadn't intended. Faster than she could keep up.

"P-Peter, I—"

"We don't have to get married right away. I don't mind waiting for you, but I can't deny my feelings anymore."

Tears burned her sinuses and spilled onto her cheeks. "Peter, slow down!"

He swiped at her cheeks with his thumbs. "Aw, sweetheart, don't cry." A soft laugh laced his voice, and he pulled her close to kiss her wet cheeks.

"Please stop, Peter. I can't—" Her thoughts scrambling, her stomach bunching, she backed out of his embrace. Suddenly cold to the bone, she tugged the corners of the quilt around her shoulders.

He furrowed his brow, his expression guarded. "What's going on, Lisa? Why are you crying?"

"You promised not to push." She waved a trembling hand and blinked hard as more tears pooled in her eyes. "Is this your idea of not rushing me?"

"You just said you had no regrets about us making love. We both wanted it."

She raked her hair back with both hands then pressed the heels of her palms into her temples. "I know. But saying you love me…talking about marriage. I'm not ready for that kind of commitment!"

He sat up slowly, his gaze wounded. "I had to be honest with you about what I feel. You're an amazing woman, Lisa, and I want to be with you, build something lasting together."

"But we can't!" Anguish sharpened the cry that wrenched from her breaking heart. "I was wrong to think we could dabble with a romance and not regret it. But I've told you from the beginning that I can't have children. My infertility ruined what had been a beautiful marriage. I can't go through the motions of a relationship that I know will end in resentment and loss again. You want more kids. You've said as much. You deserve the big family I can't give you."

He stared at her silently for long seconds, her nerves stretching tauter.

"What about adoption? Surrogacy? There are other options," he murmured.

She pinched the bridge of her nose. How many million times had she gone around this rollercoaster with Ray. Hashing and rehashing. Debating and arguing.

"Red tape keeps good parents from adopting. Surrogates grow attached to the fetus. Every option has so many potential problems and roadblocks."

"You're just borrowing trouble. That's a cop-out."

"No, it's reality, Peter. We tried to adopt once, and the biological mother changed her mind. The disappointment was devastating. It was the straw that broke Ray. He left soon after that."

"I'm so sorry, sweetheart." He stroked her cheek, his own eyes damp.

Lisa drew a deep breath for courage. "Peter, I care too

much about you to let you throw away your life with a barren woman."

Grasping her chin, he narrowed a stern but loving look on her. "Maybe you should let me decide what is right for me and my life. I love you. Just the way you are. No, it doesn't make me happy to think of never having more children, but I can deal with it."

She tugged her chin free from his grasp. "Well, I *can't* deal with it, Peter! I'm still haunted by the ghosts of my first failed marriage. I ache every day for the babies I'll never carry. I don't think I'm strong enough to survive another broken heart when the reality of my situation catches up with you." When he opened his mouth, clearly ready to deny her claim, she held up a hand to silence him. "It will catch up. Just like it caught up to Ray."

Peter tightened his jaw, his eyes dark. "I'm not Ray."

With a weary sigh, Lisa slumped her shoulders. A sense of defeat crashed down on her. With her back to the wall, she was faced with truths she couldn't outrun. "But I'm still me, and I still can't have children. Nothing has changed for *me.* I care about you, Peter, but I'm scared! I'm so afraid of winding up in the same place I found myself five years ago when Ray had enough and left me. He thought he loved me enough to wade through the pain and disappointment, too. But he was wrong." Her voice broke, and she paused long enough to wipe her tears on the corner of the quilt. "I'm scared of loving you, Peter."

Peter scowled, but his eyes reflected the pain of heartbreak. "Well, that doesn't say much for your trust in me, does it?"

"It's not you I don't trust. It's me. I don't know if I can ever be happy without my own children, and I won't drag you down in my pain."

He scrubbed his hands over his face and shoved to his

feet. Snatching up his boxers and pants, he started dressing, his motions jerky. "You know, if it were just me, I'd tell you that I had the patience to wait for you to see what we have together. I've waited ten years to find someone I loved enough to put myself out there for, so what's a few more months or years?"

A sharp ache slashed through her chest as she watched him jam his arms into the sleeves of his shirt. The scene unfolded as if under water—blurry, slow motion, surreal. In her head a voice screamed, begging her to make him stop. To go back and unsay what had been said.

"But I have to think about my son." Peter met her gaze with a pained gaze. "He's already forming bonds with you. He lost one mother already. I can't let him grow attached to you, only to have you walk away down the road because you're *afraid* of committing to me."

Afraid. The disappointment and disgust that filled his tone with that word reverberated inside her. Was she throwing away the best thing to happen to her in years because of fear? She was already planning to change her career path to avoid facing her personal pain and loneliness.

Bile churned in her gut. She was a coward, letting the best of life pass her by while she licked her wounds and mourned her misfortune. But she didn't know what else to do. She couldn't change her infertility. And she was sinking in the tar pit of her own dejection.

Peter finished dressing and pinned a penetrating stare on her. "You have to choose, Lisa. For Patrick's sake. But we can't do this halfway. I have *all* from you—or we have nothing. What will it be?"

Her heart sank. She couldn't blame him for issuing his ultimatum. He had to protect Patrick from further heartbreak.

The quilt still wrapped around her like a shield—though a worthless protection that had allowed arrows to pierce her heart—Lisa rose from the floor on shaky legs and gathered her clothes.

Her heart breaking, she gave Peter the only answer she could. "Nothing. I can't do this halfway either, Peter. And I can't promise you what I don't have in me to give."

Before he could respond, Peter's cell phone rang. The harsh tones jangled her already frayed nerves. At first she thought he'd ignore it, but after several rings, he stepped over to the end table where he'd left the cell phone and checked the caller ID.

Frowning, he flipped open the receiver and pressed it to his ear. "Hello?"

Numb with loss and trembling with regret, Lisa tugged on her jeans and bra while Peter took his call. Her head buzzed with tangled emotions.

As she pulled her sweater over her head, Peter's tone, more than his words, alerted her to trouble. She faced him and found his face pale with shock and worry.

"Do your best to calm him down. I'm on my way home." He snapped his phone closed and spun to face her. His eyes were bright with anxiety. "Get your shoes. We have to go."

Lisa's heart climbed into her throat. "What's happened?"

"A note was left on our porch, and Patrick found it." Peter's hands shook as he rammed his feet into his boots. "It was a death threat."

Chapter 13

Nothing.

Lisa's blunt response to his ultimatum echoed hollowly in Peter's head, tumbling with his mother's frightened voice. *Someone's threatened your life, Peter. Patrick found the note. He's hysterical.*

His world seemed to be crumbling, and he was at a loss what to do about any of it.

Across the cab of his truck, Lisa sat with her hands knotted together and the strain of the past half hour creasing her face. He'd offered to drop her at her house but she declined, stating that she would go crazy not knowing what was happening with Patrick.

Her interest in Patrick's well-being and concern over the death threat proved to Peter that she cared about him and his family.

She just didn't care enough to fight her fears and look for a way through the morass of her infertility. Peter's chest contracted until he couldn't breathe. Why had he let himself fall for Lisa when he knew the risk to his heart? Her skittishness about getting involved with him should have been enough warning that with her he'd end up nursing the pain of rejection and loss again.

Yet he couldn't be angry. Couldn't resent her decision. Because his heart broke for her pain. He understood the depth of her trepidation and the roots of her reluctance.

He simply had nothing that could assuage that fear and convince her to take a chance on love again.

As he pulled into his driveway, Patrick bolted through the front door and was clambering at the driver's door before Peter even had the engine shut off.

Peter stepped out of the truck, and his son threw himself against Peter.

"Dad, someone wants to k-kill you! They sent a letter with a bullet in it. You said your job wasn't dangerous. Why would someone want to hurt you? Who would want to kill you?" The flurry of questions that Patrick lobbed at him in a tear-choked voice battered Peter like fists.

He wrapped Patrick in a fierce bear hug intended to calm his son, but which he found he needed just as much to soothe his tattered nerves. He clung to Patrick, battling the sting of his own tears, the fear of something happening to Patrick, the heartache of losing Lisa, and he cherished the feel of his baby—his son—in his arms.

A feeling Lisa had never, would never experience. The grief that shot through him on Lisa's behalf nearly brought Peter to his knees. Living daily with an unrequited yearning for a baby, dealing with the neverending emptiness on top of her husband's abandonment... Peter staggered under the weight of her losses. No wonder she was so terrified of another failed relationship, of reviving the ache of being a childless couple.

"Hey, calm down," he crooned. "I'm okay, sport. No one is going to kill me. And I won't let anyone hurt you either."

Jolene crossed the yard, her face lined with stress and worry, and she handed him a folded sheet of paper. "It was taped to the front door."

With a final squeeze, he stepped back from Patrick. "Did you preserve the tape? We might get a good fingerprint off it."

She grimaced. "No. I didn't think about that. I was so worried about you and about Patrick's reaction—"

Peter stepped back from Patrick and unfolded the note. From the corner of his eye, he saw Lisa round the front of the truck and sweep his son into a firm embrace, mothering Patrick despite her breakup with Peter.

The letter had been addressed to Patrick and read, *Tell your father to butt out or he'll be the next to die.*

"Butt out," Peter muttered under his breath, the message ringing bells in his memory. Wes Colton had warned him away from his investigation with the same words.

Fury burned through Peter, vibrating in every muscle.

Had the sheriff stooped to making criminal threats to children to drive home his point?

For all his distrust of Wes Colton's handling of the murder investigation, Peter felt the sheriff didn't seem the sort to resort to such juvenile and gutless tactics of intimidation. But Peter knew with a certainty *some* Colton was behind the threat.

And his money was on Maisie.

Judging by the number of vehicles parked in the main drive of the Colton ranch, Peter guessed most of the clan had gathered for some family event. Logical, seeing as it was the day before Thanksgiving, and convenient, seeing as how he couldn't be sure which Colton was responsible for the threatening note.

Most of the lights inside the sprawling, rustic-wood ranch house were ablaze, illuminating the home like a Christmas tree at the foot of the majestic Rockies. The scene was homey, inviting…deceptive.

As he climbed out of his truck and braced himself against the stiff, cold wind, Peter reminded himself that the magnificent stained-wood-and-mountain-stone mansion housed a brood of vipers.

Remembering the terror in Patrick's eyes because of the death threat, Peter squared his shoulders and strode to the front door. His knock was answered by a young voice calling, "I'll get it!"

When the door opened, Jeremy Colton greeted Peter with a puzzled look. "Oh, uh, hi, Mr. Walsh." He looked behind Peter. "Is Patrick with you?"

Peter faltered. He hadn't counted on Jeremy witnessing his showdown with the adult Coltons. Jeremy, who was Patrick's friend. And who could easily be his own half-brother.

Acid roiled in Peter's gut. "No, Patrick's at home. Is your mother or Wes here?"

"Well, sorta. They're kinda busy. We're just about to eat a big family dinner."

So the gang was all here. Perfect.

Peter took off his gloves and jammed them in his coat pocket. "It's important that I talk to them."

"Who is it, honey?" A slim, older blond woman Peter recognized from newspaper pictures appeared in the foyer behind Jeremy. Sharon Colton, Darius's current wife in a string of many. When she spotted Peter on the porch, Sharon came up short, her expression wary. "Mr. Walsh, is…is there a problem?"

Peter glanced to Jeremy. He refused to air his wrath in front of the boy unless the Coltons gave him no choice. "Why don't you run along, Jeremy, and tell Wes and your mother I need to see them."

Jeremy sprinted away, calling, "Mom! Uncle Wes!"

Sharon gripped the edge of the door as if it were all that supported her. "What's going on, Mr. Walsh?"

The heavy thud of footsteps signaled the arrival of not one, but several, Colton men. Leading the way, Darius spotted Peter and scowled darkly. When he reached the door, he shoved his wife back into the shadows, growling, "I'll handle this, Sharon."

Sharon turned meekly and faded into the background.

Peter scanned the other faces that gathered in the foyer. Duke, Damien and Finn stood behind their father like the goon squad, ready to remove Peter bodily on cue from Darius.

"What do you want, Walsh?" Darius's voice rumbled, low and menacing, like thunder announcing an approaching storm.

Peter thrust the letter toward Darius. The patriarch was as good a place to start as any.

"I want to know which one of you bastards sent this to my son."

Darius ignored the paper Peter shoved at him and glowered. "Care to rephrase that?"

Peter returned a stony glare. "No, I don't. Because terrorizing a ten-year-old boy is the kind of vile move only a sorry coward would make. I won't stand by and let you Coltons harass my family any longer."

More family members appeared from the back rooms. Susan Kelley joined Duke, lacing her hand in his with a curious frown. Perry, Wes and Lily Masterson arrived right behind Susan. Spying Peter, Wes pushed his way to the front of the group. "What's going on?"

"Mr. Walsh was just leaving, Wes." Darius tried to shut the door on Peter, and Peter's hackles went up.

Ramming his shoulder into the door, he plowed his way into the Colton's front hall, fully aware of the angry glares and hostile stance of the many Colton alpha males. Peter didn't care if he was outnumbered. One of the Coltons had come after his son, terrorizing Patrick, making dire threats. He wouldn't let such an offense pass. "I'm not going anywhere until I know who sent this!" Again he waved the letter. He could feel his blood pressure rising, and he fought to keep it in check. He had to keep his wits about him against the Coltons. "Although I have my suspicions."

Wes took the note and read it. Furrowed his brow. "Where did you get this?"

"It was left at my house with a bullet. Patrick found it."

Darius took the note from his son, and Damien and Duke crowded closer to read over his shoulder.

Wes braced his hands on his hips. "I'll need that bullet, too. I'll start an investigation, if you want."

"You won't have to look far. Ask Maisie what she knows about it."

"Maisie?" Darius asked.

Peter faced the patriarch. "Do you know that she had an affair with my father back in 1995? I have reason to believe Jeremy is my father's son."

The women gasped softly, and a murmur of discontent rose amongst the men.

"I'm aware of Maisie's mistake," Darius said coolly, confirming Peter's suspicions. The man's face remained hard, emotionless.

"What does that have to do with this note?" Wes asked.

"Why don't you ask her?" Peter divided a dark look between Darius and Wes. "A spurned lover could have reason to murder, to seek revenge. Especially if she's trying to cover her tracks, hide an illicit affair, the paternity of an illegitimate son."

An uneasy silence filled the foyer until Darius bellowed, "Maisie!"

The clop of hard-soled shoes sounded in the hall, and Maisie pulled up short when she saw her family clustered around Peter. "What's all this about?"

Darius thrust the letter in her direction. "What do you know about a death threat sent to Patrick Walsh?"

Maisie stiffened. Her hands balled at her sides. "Why are you accusing me?" her tone grew shrill.

As she shuffled cautiously forward, her brothers and their girlfriends parted to let Maisie through.

Peter regarded Maisie with a narrowed gaze. Disgust and fury churned in his gut. "I think you know. Your secret is out, Maisie. Jeremy is Mark Walsh's son, isn't he? Did you kill my father to keep him from telling the world your dirty little secret?"

Maisie drew a sharp breath, her eyes widening in horror. "How did you find out? You can't—"

In an instant, her shock morphed to rage. With a keening, animalistic wail, she charged at Peter. She attacked him, arms swinging, fingernails raking, feet flailing. A blur of fury and wrath, vicious strikes and battering kicks. "I hate you! I hate you! You've ruined everything! You'll pay for this!"

Wes bit out a scorching obscenity and, with Damien's help, peeled Maisie off Peter. Finn stepped forward to help subdue Maisie, who fought their hold like a rabid wildcat.

Stunned, but not really surprised by Maisie's outburst and attack, Peter dabbed at his bloody lip, where Maisie had clawed him with her fingernails. His cheek throbbed, and his shins ached from her assault, and he'd likely have a shiner in the morning thanks to a well-placed jab.

With his brothers restraining Maisie, Wes stepped toward her and pointed to the note with the death threat Darius still held. "Did you send Patrick Walsh that threat, Maisie?"

Her eyes narrowed on Peter with a venomous glare. "Yes!" she hissed. "I hope all of the Walshes die! They're nothing but heartless animals."

Wes closed his eyes, and his shoulders drooped wearily. Finn and Duke exchanged guarded looks.

"First Lucy betrays Damien and stomps on his heart," Maisie continued ranting, red-faced with anger, "then Mark knocks me up and tells me to get an abortion when he finds out. He never really cared about me. He just used me and abandoned me! The cold-hearted rat deserved to die!"

Peter shuddered. He might be bleeding and bruised, but he had what he wanted. The truth.

He turned to Wes with a level gaze. "Your sister assaulted me. She's admitted to sending a death threat to my son and murdering my father." He aimed a finger at Maisie. "I want her arrested."

"What!" she shrieked. "No! Wes, you can't—"

Wes held up a hand to hush his sister. "I can charge her with battery and sending the threat, but I didn't hear a murder confession."

"Neither did I," Damien added. His brothers shook their heads in agreement.

Peter raised his chin and moved toward Wes. "Sounds

like you should add her to your suspect list at least." He gritted his teeth and cast a side glance to the grim faces around him. "I told you if you'd look at your own family you could solve my father's murder and the other attacks on my family without your lengthy investigation."

Wes shot a glance to his sister. "Did you kill Mark Walsh, Maisie?"

"No!" She struggled against the hands that still held her.

Wes arched an eyebrow. "Maisie didn't kill anyone. This changes nothing about my investigation."

Peter tensed. "Bring her in for attacking me then. I'm pressing charges for assault."

Maisie grunted indignantly and cut her gaze to Darius, who stood back, arms folded over his chest, watching the proceedings with a disapproving glower. "Dad, you can't let him do that!"

"Lily, call my office, please," Wes said, "Ask them to send a cruiser out here." He sighed and faced his sister. "Maisie, you have the right to remain silent—"

"Wes, no!" Maisie sent another pleading look to her father. "Daddy, please! Do something! This town owes you. You can't let them arrest me!"

"You made this bed for yourself. Now lie in it." Darius shoved the threatening letter toward Wes then strode into the bowels of his ranch house.

Damien squared his shoulders and moved to block Peter's view of Wes reading Maisie her rights, of Maisie crying and begging her brothers to let her go. "You've done enough damage here tonight. I think you should go." His tone, black glare and rigid stance left no doubt his suggestion was actually an order.

Swiping a trickle of blood from his mouth and rolling the ache of tension from his shoulders, Peter gave Damien a curt nod. "I'll go. But your family hasn't heard the last of me. I won't rest until I know which one of you killed my father and declared war on my family."

"Planning to railroad through false charges like your family did against me?" Damien asked, his tone bitter.

"No, this time I'll make sure we get the right person, and I'll see that the charges stick." Turning on his heel, Peter stormed through the front door and across the lawn to his truck, parked at the far end of the driveway.

As he passed one of the bunkhouses where several ranch hands had gathered outside for a smoke, the sound of Maisie protesting her arrest to Wes in shrill tones wafted through the November chill. The ranch hands shook their heads, and Peter heard one man say, "Just goes to show—money can't buy happiness."

"You can't pick your family, but I bet ol' Sheriff Wes sure wishes he could right about now," another hand added with a scoff.

Peter paused with his hand on the door handle of his truck and looked back up at the main house. The Coltons spilled out the front door as Wes took Maisie out to meet the arriving patrol car.

You can't pick your family...

Or could you?

As Peter pulled onto the highway that led back to Honey Creek, the old ranch hand's statement tumbled in his head, tangling with a collage of snapshot memories of his own family. His heartache over Lisa's choice to end their relationship without giving it a fair chance. Patrick's haunted expression over the death threat when he'd arrived home this afternoon. Mark Walsh's womanizing and disinterest in his wife and children. Mary's and Lucy's newfound happiness with upstanding men who would love and protect them. Craig Warner filling the role of father for Peter in recent years. Katie's death as she gave Peter the greatest gift in his life, his son.

Peter hadn't chosen some members of his family, wouldn't wish his absentee lothario father on anyone. Yet he'd chosen his young bride, just as Mary had chosen Jake. Lucy had chosen Steve.

He'd chosen to count Craig as a father figure, and Craig treated him like an adopted son.

Adopted.

Peter tightened his hands on the steering wheel, and his heart pounded harder.

We tried to adopt once, and the biological mother changed her mind. The disappointment was devastating. It was the straw that broke Ray.

Earlier today, he'd been so caught up in Lisa's pain, his own emotions and desperation to change Lisa's mind that he hadn't fully analyzed all the ramifications of their situation. He'd been so confident in his own feelings for Lisa, so cocksure about their future that he hadn't given real thought to how to make it work. Lisa needed that reassurance, not ultimatums.

Peter squeezed his eyes shut and cursed his blindness and stupidity.

He prayed she'd still be at his house when he arrived. They couldn't leave things unsettled between them.

Jolene met him at the door. Her troubled expression asked what she didn't verbalize.

"Maisie admitted sending the note," he told her in soft tones before going inside. "I was right about her having an affair with Dad. Jeremy is his son."

"Why are you bleeding?" Jolene reached for the cut on his lip, and Peter pulled away.

"She attacked me when I told her the secret was out.

She swears she didn't kill Dad, but her assault on me and the threatening note were enough to have her arrested."

"Wes allowed his sister to be arrested?" Jolene sounded stunned.

"He's the one who took her into custody...until his backup arrived."

Jolene touch a hand to her temple. "I'm so ready for all this drama to be behind us. You know, years ago, the Walshes and the Coltons were friends. I miss those days." She sighed and shook her head, then raised a firmly loving gaze to Peter. "Enough dwelling on our troubles. Thanksgiving is about counting our blessings. And the Walshes have plenty. Craig is stronger every day. Mary and Lucy have never been happier. And you have a healthy, growing son. And Lisa—"

His heart twisted. Hadn't Lisa filled his mom in on their break-up?

"Mom, about Lisa..."

Jolene gave him a quelling look and put a finger to her lips. "Shh. Come here. There's something you need to see."

Wes rocked back in his desk chair waiting to hear from his deputy that Maisie had been processed, printed and photographed. What a night!

Maisie had always been a handful for their parents. The oldest child and only girl in the family until Joan had come along when Maisie was fifteen, Maisie had been spoiled yet also strangely isolated among all those Colton sons, especially after her mother had died when she was five. With her unrivaled beauty, men twice her age had showered her with the wrong kind of attention at too early an age. Yet Maisie had sought more and more outrageous ways to attract attention from her family. She'd pushed every envelope, courted danger and invited scandal but, to Wes's knowledge, had never crossed the line of legality. Until tonight.

He rubbed his chest where a raw ache had settled. He hated bringing Maisie in, but what choice had he had? She'd admitted to threatening Peter Walsh's life, had viciously attacked him. His sister was out of control, headed for a bigger fall if he didn't intervene.

Like he needed something else to worry about. This mess with Mark Walsh's murder, Craig Warner's poisoning, money-laundering schemes that had brought the FBI to his tiny town...the stress wore on him. Something had to break soon.

"Sheriff, your sister is in the interrogation room," one of his deputies said from the door. "She's asked to see you."

Wes nodded. "Thanks."

Bracing his hands on his desk, he shoved to his feet, feeling far older than his thirty-three years tonight.

Maisie had her head buried in arms folded on the table when he walked in and sat across from her. She raised a teary gaze to him, her luminous aqua eyes rimmed in red, lined with distress and fatigue. Despite her taller-than-average height, his sister seemed smaller tonight, child-like, drawn into herself, vulnerable.

Wes's chest clenched. "What's going on with you, Maisie? What possessed you to send Patrick Walsh that death threat against his father?"

She swiped at her cheek and shook her head slowly. "I don't know, Wes. I was in town earlier today, picking up a few last-minute things for our dinner, getting an early start on my Christmas shopping..." She lowered her gaze to the table where she restlessly twisted a used facial tissue. "Everywhere I went, people told me Peter Walsh had been asking about me last week. Did anyone know who Jeremy's father was? Did anyone remember who I'd been involved with in 1995? Could Mark Walsh be Jeremy's father?"

Her hands trembled, and she shredded the tissue into bits. "If I'd wanted people to know the mistake I'd made with Mark Walsh years ago, I'd have told people myself. But I never wanted anyone to know that that cretin, Mark Walsh, was my son's dad. I never wanted Jeremy to have to live with that burden."

Wes leaned forward and placed a calming hand over Maisie's fidgeting fingers. "Go on. What did you do then?"

"I got mad. I'd heard you complain earlier about how he was nosing around in the death of his father and could jeopardize your investigation. I knew he had to be stopped. I knew a warning would be ignored. He hadn't listened to you after all. So I thought…if I involved Patrick—"

Wes frowned and squeezed Maisie's hand. "Patrick Walsh is just a kid, Maisie. How would you feel if someone sent a letter like that to Jeremy?"

Her eyes filled with fresh tears. "I'd hate it. I never wanted to hurt Patrick. He seems like a sweet kid—despite being a Walsh. But I didn't think—"

"Yeah. You didn't think." Wes gritted his teeth. "And now look where your temper has gotten you. You'll have plenty of time to think tonight. I've got to put you in the holding cell until your bond comes through."

As he scooted his chair back and stood, Maisie's shoulders slumped.

"Wes?" Her voice cracked, high and thin, full of pain.

Wes stopped at the door and faced his sister. "Yeah, Mais."

"Damien is talking about leaving town. Going to Nevada to start over."

Wes sighed. He hated to see Damien leave when the family had only just gotten him back. "Yeah, I know."

"I think that may be what I should do, too." Maisie lifted her aqua eyes, puddled with tears. "I have a horrible reputation in this town that I won't soon lose. Being a Colton in Honey Creek is hard. People expect so much, watch your every move, talk about you as if you don't have feelings. I should move far from here and make a fresh start."

"Are you sure? You'd be uprooting Jeremy from everything and everyone he's ever known."

"Maybe that's not such a bad thing. I don't want him living under the pressures I've known living here." She tucked her hair behind her ear. "Don't we have some cousins in Texas?"

"I think so. But…you know you can't leave town until these new charges against you are settled."

Maisie closed her eyes slowly and sighed. "I know." She rubbed her temple and said softly, "Go home, Wes. Lily's waiting for you."

Peter followed his mother into the living room. She put her finger on her lips, signaling for him to be quiet, then pointed to his sofa.

Under a shared quilt, Patrick lay huddled against Lisa, his head on her shoulder, her arms around him. They were both asleep.

The touching scene wrenched Peter's heart. Patrick needed a mother. Lisa needed a child. The solution seemed so obvious, but how did he convince Lisa to step out on faith, to give their love a chance? Her pain was deep and stubborn.

He took a step toward them, but Jolene caught his arm,

crooked a finger to motion him to the kitchen. Again he followed, curious.

Jake Pierson and Mary sat at his kitchen table nursing mugs of hot tea, their expressions grim.

Peter wasn't sure he could take any more bad news tonight. His world was already falling apart, his heart broken, his child terrorized. "What's going on?"

He heard the shuffle of feet as his mother backed out of the room, giving them privacy to talk.

Jake spoke first. "I hear you paid a visit to the Colton ranch tonight."

"My life had been threatened. My child scared witless. I couldn't sit back and do nothing."

"You could have called the authorities, Peter."

"Not when the authorities are the problem. Wes is a Colton. They're the ones behind all this. Maisie admitted to sending the note."

Mary frowned. "Just the same, there are proper channels for this kind of thing, so that citizens don't go off half-cocked seeking vigilante justice."

Peter sighed heavily. "So you came to lecture me? 'Cause I'm not in the mood."

"No," Jake said. "We came to level with you, before you do real damage to this case."

Peter tensed, raised his chin. "Level with me?"

Mary nodded. "But you have to keep this in the strictest confidence. Please, Peter. It's critical to the case that nothing leak about what's going on behind the scenes. Do you hear me? Do you understand?"

Apprehension stirred a drumbeat in his chest. "Talk to me."

Jake and Mary exchanged a troubled look.

"Your father's murder may be related to other crimes

that the FBI is investigating," Jake said. "Same with Craig's poisoning. You're right that they are probably linked."

Peter pulled out a chair and sat without breaking eye contact with Jake. "What kind of other crimes?"

"Money-laundering, real-estate fraud, a whole list of smaller related charges." Jake turned his mug idly and shook his head. "We don't know yet how it all fits together, but Wes has been cooperating with the FBI and their undercover investigators now for months."

"When we started digging, asking questions, we became a target," Mary said. "Remember when Jake's partner was killed? We think the murderer was really after Jake. The attempt on our lives a few days later cinched it for us. The case wasn't worth our lives, not when we'd just found each other and had a chance for real happiness."

"The FBI has someone in place, an undercover operative who can bust this case wide open in time." Jake tapped the table with his finger to emphasize his point. "But you have to back off. You can't interfere. You could ruin everything, right when Wes and the FBI are nearly ready to make arrests."

Wes had said much the same thing the last time Peter confronted him. *Walsh, this case is bigger than just a murder investigation...*

"Who is the undercover agent?" Peter looked to Jake. "You?"

Jake shook his head as Mary said, "We don't know who, don't care who, as long as it all gets settled. Soon. We trust Wes, Peter. He's a good lawman."

Peter propped his elbows on the table and raked both hands through his hair. "Why didn't you tell me this sooner?"

"It's classified. We shouldn't be telling you now, but when you go off and confront the Coltons at their ranch..." Mary heaved a sigh. "We asked you to drop your investigation weeks ago. For your safety as well as Patrick's. If what we've told you tonight isn't enough to convince you to leave this case to the authorities, then think about Patrick. Don't you want him to be able to sleep at night without fearing his father will be shot or run off the road or poisoned?"

Peter thought of his son, already facing the heartache of losing Lisa thanks to their break-up. He raised his gaze to Mary and Jake. The decision was easy.

"All right. I'll drop my investigation."

Jake gave a satisfied nod. "I'll try to keep you informed, but honestly we don't know that much ourselves now that we've backed off. I trust Wes and the FBI, Peter. And you can too."

Peter drew a cleansing breath. "Let's hope so."

Careful not to disturb the sleeping pair, Peter sat on the edge of the couch. He studied the tear tracks on his son's cheeks, and his stomach bunched. Patrick had needed comfort tonight, and his father had not been there for him. Peter had let his grudge against the Coltons get the better of him. Making a scene, disturbing a family holiday meal, all to satisfy his own sense of retribution.

Thank God Lisa had stayed. Not that Jolene couldn't have handled Patrick's tears, but his mother had been through so much recently herself. And Patrick had really bonded with Lisa.

...is it okay if I call you Mom?

Peter curled his hand into a fist of frustration. He had to change Lisa's mind about ending their relationship. Somehow.

You can't pick your family...

The old ranch hand was wrong. You *could* pick the people you loved, the people you surrounded yourself with, the people who became your family, even if not by blood.

Patrick had chosen Lisa to be his mother. And Peter wanted her as his wife. Needed her. Loved her more than anything—except his son.

Taking a deep breath and saying a prayer that he'd find the right words, he stroked Lisa's cheek and whispered, "Hey, Sleeping Beauty. I'm home."

Her eyelids fluttered open, and a smile graced her lips briefly before shadows crept into her gaze. "Are you all right? Your face—"

"Turns out Maisie Colton has a vicious right hook."

"Peter…"

"I'm okay. Help me get this guy to his bed. We need to talk."

A wary concern narrowed her eyes as Peter jostled Patrick lightly. "Wake up, sport. I'd carry you to your bed, but you've gotten kinda big for that."

Patrick grunted and rolled away from Peter.

"Patrick." Peter jostled his son again, and this time Patrick's eyes sprang open and he bolted up, alarm on his face.

"Dad? Did you find the guy who sent the letter? Are you okay?"

He tousled Patrick's hair and helped him up from the couch. "Everything's fine. No one is going to hurt you or me. I promise."

"Or Mom…I mean, Ms. Navarre?"

Peter's gaze darted to Lisa's. She bit down on her bottom lip, her eyes sad.

"I intend to keep all of us safe." Peter's gaze included Lisa. "No matter what. Okay, sport?"

Patrick nodded sleepily, his eyelids drooping again. Peter ushered his son to bed, kissed his forehead and bade him goodnight before returning to the living room. His mother puttered about his kitchen, still discreetly giving him time and space to sort things out with Lisa.

Lisa sat on the edge of the sofa, putting her shoes back on as if preparing to leave. "If you would drive me home, Peter, I'll get out of your hair and—"

"Don't go." He wrapped his fingers around her wrist, halting her progress. "Please talk to me."

"I don't know what we have left to say. You asked me to decide on *all* or *nothing*, for Patrick's sake. And I saw tonight why you had to make that call. Patrick doesn't deserve to have his heart broken. He's an impressionable boy who needs a mother and I—"

"He needs *you,* Lisa. He's bonded with you. Just like I have." He squeezed her hand, his expression pleading. "We love you."

Tears bloomed in her eyes. "Peter, don't make this harder than it already is."

He swiped moisture from her cheek and locked his gaze with hers. "Listen to me. I was wrong to give you an ultimatum. I see that now. I have no excuse except…I wanted assurance that we were both dedicated to making our relationship work…because I want us to work so desperately. But instead of supporting you and giving you the understanding you needed in facing the pain from your past, I pressured you and forced you to make a hard choice. I'm so sorry, sweetheart."

She flashed a weak, sad smile. "Apology accepted. But—"

"No. Not *but.* I learned something else tonight. Figured it out really…" He captured her face between his hands. "I overheard a comment that made me really think about what family is, who my family is, why we love our family. And blood is only a small part of deciding who we love."

Her brow wrinkled. "Peter, what does this have to do with us?"

"Everything. My dad was related to me by blood, but Craig Warner is more a father to me than Mark Walsh ever was. Patrick wants so badly to call you Mom, because he sees you in that role, wants you to be his mother. He loves you, even though there is no blood relationship."

Lisa's chin trembled as new tears spilled from her eyelashes. "I love him too. He's a great kid, Peter. But I—"

"Please, Lisa. Stop saying *but*. I know you're scared, but I'm not ready to give up on us. Think about what we could have together. We *are* a family—you, me and Patrick."

Her expression grew more wistful, more pained.

"And we can adopt more children. If you're worried about a birth mother changing her mind, then we'll adopt children already in the system, kids who are desperate for the kind of love we can offer."

She was softening. He saw the yearning that flashed brightly in her eyes.

"We *can* choose our family. I chose Craig to be my father figure. Patrick chose you to be his mother. And we can choose to adopt children who need us as much as we need them. Maybe they'll be babies, maybe not. But we will adopt as many children as you want. I swear it."

She began to shake, and he pressed her trembling hands between his. "The…approval process can be long and full of red tape."

He heard the years of dejection and frustration in her voice, still holding her back.

"Good thing I'm a stubborn and persistent man then."

She grinned finally, laughing through her tears. "You are that!"

Peter framed her face in his hands and touched his

forehead to hers. "And I choose you, Lisa Navarre, to be my wife. I want you to grow old with me, no matter what else happens in our lives."

She drew a quick, shallow breath and curled her fingers into his hair. "Oh, Peter…"

"If we never have any children besides Patrick, I will still be happy as long as you are beside me. And I will do everything in my power to make you happy until your dying day. I love you as you are. And if you give me a chance, I'll show you how much every day for the rest of our lives."

She grew still, her gaze searching his as if assessing his sincerity. "You still want me, even knowing what my infertility will mean in our marriage?"

He gave her a quick kiss. "Unlike Ray, I'm prepared to stand by you, support you, be a team, even through whatever bad times may come our way. Marry me, Lisa. We belong together. I want to build a family with you."

Lisa felt her world tilt as the possibilities Peter was offering her sank in and shifted her whole perspective on her future. Adopt children with Peter? Be Patrick's mother? Grow old with Peter at her side?

In a matter of hours, minutes really, she'd gone from facing dismally lonely days of heartache without the man she loved to a bright future with everything she'd dreamed of and wanted. Because of Peter. The man she loved. The man with whom she wanted to build a home.

The answer was clear, but she hesitated. She'd had her hopes dashed so many times, and as wonderful as Peter's proposal was, she had to be sure she wasn't dreaming.

Peter's brow puckered in a frown. "That's an awfully serious face, Lisa. What's wrong?"

"I just have to be sure… I—" She lifted her chin and laid a hand along his cheek. "Kiss me, Peter."

"Gladly." He caught her lips with his, and she wrapped her arms around his neck, holding him close, as if she'd never let him go. Because she had no intention of letting this loving man out of her life. His lips stirred a sweet hunger inside her, but more important, his kiss touched the vulnerable part of her soul, a place she'd spent years protecting.

She wasn't dreaming, and she wasn't alone anymore.

She sagged against him, feeling the weight of the world lift from her. Her arms tightened around him, and she whispered, "I choose you, too, Peter. I love you, and I want very much to be part of your family."

Peter held her as she cried happy tears. "Consider it done."

Epilogue

Later that night, Wes returned to his office, eager to wrap up the paperwork associated with Maisie's arrest and get back home to Lily and their interrupted family dinner. Several minutes later, a knock roused him from his work, and Damien opened Wes's office door a few inches and slipped inside. "Got a minute?"

Wes shrugged. "I guess. You here to post Maisie's bond?"

"That, and…we need to talk." As Damien took a seat in a visitor's chair, his brother's dark gaze sent a chill through Wes.

"Can this wait until we get home?"

A muscle in Damien's jaw flexed as he ground his back teeth. "No. It's official business."

Wes set his pen aside and leaned forward. "Okay. You have my attention. What's this about?"

"It's about the person responsible for all that's been

happening around Honey Creek lately. Mark Walsh's murder, Craig Warner's poisoning, the money-laundering—" Damien's expression darkened. "I think I know who is behind all of it."

*See below for a sneak peek from our classic
Harlequin® Romance® line.*

Introducing DADDY BY CHRISTMAS by Patricia Thayer.

MIA caught sight of Jarrett when he walked into the open
lobby. It was hard not to notice the man. In a charcoal
business suit with a crisp white shirt and striped tie covered
by a dark trench coat, he looked more Wall Street than
small-town Colorado.

Mia couldn't blame him for keeping his distance. He
was probably tired of taking care of her.

Besides, why would a man like Jarrett McKane be
interested in her? Why would he want to take on a woman
expecting a baby? Yet he'd done so many things for her.
He'd been there when she'd needed him most. How could
she not care about a man like that?

Heart pounding in her ears, she walked up behind him.
Jarrett turned to face her. "Did you get enough sleep last
night?"

"Yes, thanks to you," she said, wondering if he'd thought
about their kiss. Her gaze went to his mouth, then she
quickly glanced away. "And thank you for not bringing up
my meltdown."

Jarrett couldn't stop looking at Mia. Blue was definitely
her color, bringing out the richness of her eyes.

"What meltdown?" he said, trying hard to focus on what
she was saying. "You were just exhausted from lack of
sleep and worried about your baby."

He couldn't help remembering how, during the night,
he'd kept going in to watch her sleep. How strange was
that? "I hope you got enough rest."

She nodded. "Plenty. And you're a good neighbor for

coming to my rescue."

He tensed. Neighbor? *What neighbor kisses you like I did?* "That's me, just the full-service landlord," he said, trying to keep the sarcasm out of his voice. He started to leave, but she put her hand on his arm.

"Jarrett, what I meant was you went beyond helping me." Her eyes searched his face. "I've asked far too much of you."

"Did you hear me complain?"

She shook her head. "You should. I feel like I've taken advantage."

"Like I said, I haven't minded."

"And I'm grateful for everything…"

Grasping her hand on his arm, Jarrett leaned forward. The memory of last night's kiss had him aching for another. "I didn't do it for your gratitude, Mia."

Gorgeous tycoon Jarrett McKane has never believed in Christmas—but he can't help being drawn to soon-to-be-mom Mia Saunders! Christmases past were spent alone…and now Jarrett may just have a fairy-tale ending for all his Christmases future!

Available December 2010, only from Harlequin® Romance®.

HREXP1210

Spotlight on
Classic

Quintessential, modern love stories
that are romance at its finest.

See the next page
to enjoy a sneak peek from
the Harlequin® Romance series.

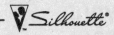

SILHOUETTE

SPECIAL EDITION

USA TODAY BESTSELLING AUTHOR

MARIE FERRARELLA

BRINGS YOU ANOTHER
HEARTWARMING STORY FROM

When Lilli McCall disappeared on him
after he proposed, Kullen Manetti swore
never to fall in love again. Eight years later
Lilli is back in his life, threatening to break
down all the walls he's put up to
safeguard his heart.

UNWRAPPING
THE PLAYBOY

*Available December
wherever books are sold.*

REQUEST YOUR FREE BOOKS!

2 FREE NOVELS
PLUS
2 FREE GIFTS!

ROMANTIC SUSPENSE

Sparked by Danger, Fueled by Passion.